STEP

S&M #1

ROXIE RIVERA

Night Works Books
College Station, Texas

Night Works Books
3515-B Longmire Drive #103
College Station, Texas 77845
www.roxierivera.com

STEP/Roxie Rivera -- 1st ed.
ISBN 978-1-63042-031-4

CHAPTER ONE

STEP

Pussy.

One word. Five letters.

The sweet pink currency that fueled the backstage

hookup market.

And right now I wanted some.

I wanted it *bad*. I wanted to be buried balls-deep in two or three of the hottest fucking groupies I could find. I wanted to get up to some real deviant shit tonight. Hot, filthy, sheet-ripping, bed-breaking fucking. I planned to ring in my birthday with a night I would never forget.

Slick with sweat from an extended set, I reached up to rake my fingers through my long hair but encountered the short bristles of my new haircut. It threw me off for a moment. The modified Mohawk with the sides buzzed short and top trimmed low had been a spur of the moment decision I had made in a fit of frustration a few mornings ago. My constantly cracking voice and aching throat were getting on my last damned nerve.

I scratched my fingernails along my scalp. I didn't exactly regret the move to hack off a decade's worth of hair growth, but I was still getting used to the strange, light feeling up top. At least my voice had performed well tonight. I had gotten through the entire set without a single wobble or crack. Hell, maybe that overpaid specialist of mine knew what the hell he was talking about after all.

Now, if I could just tackle that *other* embarrassing problem of mine, I would be fucking golden.

I headed down the steps leading away from the stage and down into the pit-like backstage of The Slaughterhouse. I owned the notorious club that catered to the goth and metal heads of Houston. We had just played an exclusive show to give our fans a taste of the new album we would be launching with a worldwide tour at the beginning of next year. The crowd had gone fucking crazy for the new songs.

Throat sore and dry, I snatched a beer from a passing waitress and took a long pull of the cold, bitter brew. It soothed the ache in my raw throat. In the back of my head, I could hear my otolaryngologist screaming at me to put the fucking alcohol down and pick up a bottle of water. Being a hard-headed asshole, I took another even longer drink of the icy beer.

Glancing back, I found my bandmates hot on my heels. Dom Rivera, Sinister Mayhem's bassist, grabbed a towel from a roadie and wiped the beading sweat from his shaved head. Tres, his younger brother and our band's head of security, kept a well-trained eye on the throng of groupies and entertainment media reps pushing forward. With one stern look, the former Marine sent them all scuttling back.

After grinding on taut strings for nearly two hours, Leif Hansson stretched his cramping fingers before gathering his blond hair into a low ponytail at the back of his neck. His younger brother, Tor, stormed by him with drumsticks still clenched in his fists. Like a damned Viking on a rampage, he shoved his way through the crowd and disappeared into one of the private halls of the labyrinthine backstage area.

I wasn't sure what the fuck was up with Tor lately, but he had been a serious bastard to everyone. I met Leif's concerned gaze across the crowd and frowned at him. Leif shrugged his tattooed shoulders and then turned away from me and into the adoring arms of two female fans with some of the best damned ink I had ever seen. I stepped to the side for a better look at the artwork adorning their skin. In those tiny leather skirts and skimpy tops, they both flashed a great deal of beautifully decorated flesh. My approving gaze landed on our band's logo stamped on their left shoulders.

"Step!" An excited and familiar female voice cut through the background noise. "Happy Birthday!"

I turned just in time to catch Hadley Rivera, Tres and Dom's little sister, as she launched herself at me. I didn't miss the grim set to her boyfriend's mouth at the sight of his girlfriend leaping onto me. I bit back the urge to make a show of giving her a big, noisy kiss because the guy was a highly decorated sniper who had been a fucking legend in the Marine Corps. I didn't want to be on the bad side of a dude who probably knew fifty different and extremely painful ways to end me.

Hadley loudly kissed my cheek. "Happy birthday, my big, Russian, tattooed almost-brother!"

With a bark of laughter, I hugged her tight but tried not to squeeze too hard. It had only been six weeks or so since her heart surgery, and I worried I might accidentally harm her still healing chest. Carefully setting her down,

I ignored the jealous onlookers who were wondering who the hell this spunky dark-haired girl with startling gray eyes was to me. I placed my hands on her shoulders and examined her from head to toe. She seemed thinner but looked healthy and happy. "Shit, it's good to see you, Hadley! How are you feeling?"

"Good." She assured me before reaching back to grasp her boyfriend's hand. With a quick tug, she silently beckoned him to join us. "The warden here gave me a pass for good behavior."

I glanced at Finn Connolly and held out my hand. "It's good to see you again, Finn."

"Step." He had a strong handshake and offered a clipped nod. "That was a hell of a show."

"Thanks, man." I wasn't sure if that was a compliment or not. Knowing what I did of Finn, the last concert this guy had attended had probably been one of Toby Keith's USO shows. The doom metal scene was an entirely different world. As if to prove my point, four luscious and scantily clad exotic dancers crossed the backstage area and head toward the VIP lounge up on the second floor of the converted trucking warehouse. I caught Finn frowning at the sight of them and decided to needle him a little. "You guys want to come up for the after-party?"

Cracking like a gunshot, Finn's answer came half of a heartbeat later. "No."

I squashed the amused smile that tugged at the corners of my mouth. "You guys sure? Once the alcohol starts flowing, those girls are going to be up on the tables. It's a show you don't want to miss." I grinned at Hadley and leaned down to tease her. "Maybe I'll finally convince you to let your hair down, sweetness."

"Our baby sister lets down one strand of her hair, and Tres and I are going to make a show of kicking your ass from one end of this club to the other," Dom growled as he butted into the conversation. He jammed his shoulder against mine with enough force that I lurched forward. "When we're done with you, Finn gets his turn."

"Shit, Dom!" I rubbed at my stinging arm. "It was just a joke."

Ignoring me, Dom reached out and gave Hadley's hair a playful tug. "Munchie, what were you doing out in the crowd? You could have been crushed."

She rolled her eyes at her older brother's overprotectiveness. "Tres and the rest of the bouncers formed a bubble around me. I couldn't even see the stage unless Finn picked me up!"

Dom grunted. "You drinking enough water, Munchie? It's hot as hell back here. You're still on the Lasix, right?"

"Yes, and yes." She sighed dramatically and gestured toward Finn. "My bodyguard has been monitoring my water intake and making sure I'm taking my meds. I'm fine. *Really*."

"She's been a model patient and has more than earned this night out." Finn draped his arm around her shoulders and leaned down to kiss the top of her head.

The tender moment between the couple caused a strange pang right in the center of my chest. I ignored the unwanted sensation and suppressed the troubling thoughts it kicked off by turning my attention to that thick, fine ass of the dark-haired looker who had just strolled by us. I decided to keep tabs on that one. She had just made my short-list of hookup possibilities.

"No, I think we're going to call it a night and head back to the penthouse," Hadley was saying when my attention reverted to the conversation.

Dom's expression turned squeamish when he jumped to the obvious conclusion about why his little sister and her boyfriend were leaving early. Apparently, Hadley's doc had given her the all-clear to get horizontal with that Marine of hers. I wanted to laugh at the look on Dom's face, but my arm still stung from the muscled bassist's last punch so I bit back the urge to be a jackass.

"Will you make sure Coby gets home safe?" Hadley tapped her brother's forearm, her fingers dancing over the intricate sleeve-work he sported. "She told me not to worry about her but…"

Dom glanced back at the pixie-sized DJ who was chatting with Slaughterhouse's events manager and gesturing animatedly toward the front of the house. He frowned. "That girl needs to get her driver's license. As flush as she is now, there's no reason for her not to buy a car or hire a damned driver and bodyguard."

Professional jealousy reared its ugly head when I considered how much cash Coby had hauled in with her outrageously popular dance remixes and that latest trap album. She had agreed to DJ tonight's party for free because we all ran in the same circle of Houston musicians, but our manager had let it slip that she was pocketing six figures a night for private parties. Six fucking figures, man! Doom metal made my blood run hot and my heart pound with excitement—but shit. I wouldn't say no to some lucrative deals like those.

"I will make sure she gets home safely." Dom gestured toward their brother. "Come on. Tres will want to see you two before you disappear."

Hadley glanced back and waved at me as her older brother led them away. The hard partying crowd tried to swallow me up, but I needed a few moments alone in the dressing room. I managed to weave my way out of the crowd and into the private hallway that two bouncers guarded. I slipped inside my dressing room and dropped into a chair.

Head in my hands, I exhaled a long and slow breath.

I hated to be ungrateful for all the success we had achieved, but sometimes it was too much. As the face of our band, I was expected to constantly interact with fans. I couldn't storm off and be a dickhead like Tor or scare people off with a glare like Dom. I didn't get to fuck everything that walked on two legs like Leif. No, I had to be the mostly responsible one.

But right now? Tonight? I wanted to run the fuck away. I wanted to close myself off in my quiet downtown penthouse apartment, have a couple of drinks and get some much needed sleep.

But I couldn't do that. No, the lead singer version of me was expected to ring in his third decade on this earth with pure debauchery. I was expected to tear up a hotel suite, fuck a string of hot, wild groupies and wake up naked in a swimming pool.

The only problem with that scenario? The years of partying hard and treating my body like shit were starting to catch up with me. After the laryngitis scare earlier in the year, I had lost some of my usual confidence and swagger.

And my ability to get hard.

Fuck, even admitting it to myself was humiliating! How the hell did that happen? How did I go from being a champion in the bedroom to relying on that bottle of blue pills in my bag? I was surrounded by hot, tight, juicy fan pussy but my cock wasn't in it.

Not tonight, I thought with a clenched jaw. Tonight? Tonight I was going to reclaim my inner porn star. I was going to take that blue pill, find a strong, wild woman to take back to my hotel suite and fuck dirty and hot until sunrise.

My mind made up, I shoved out of my chair and strode to my bag on the vanity counter. I found the bottle of pills prescribed to an alias and shook one out onto my palm. I knocked it back with a drink from my water bottle and returned to my party.

By now, Coby—or DJ Cobalt as she was known when spinning—had the crowd pumped. Not surprisingly, she had created a special set for Slaughterhouse, mixing trap and electronic with goth and metal. How she managed to make it sound so damned good perplexed me. That girl had a gift, and I was in awe of it.

After an hour of fan photos and autographs and knocking back the endless stream of drinks that were offered to me, I was dragged up to the VIP lounge where an obscene birthday cake waited for me. Dom and Coby led the crowd in singing *Happy Birthday*, and I made a big show of making my wish and blowing out my candles. I ate the obligatory piece, downed another drink, made the rounds and then decided I had had enough.

Ready to make my escape for a private party of my own, I scanned the throng of groupies panting for a chance to get their greedy little fingers inside my leather pants. Like a kid surrounded by gifts on Christmas morning, I didn't know where to start. Suddenly my plan to find one gorgeous, fun woman altered drastically. One for each decade sounded much better.

There were vamps in fetish wear, their bodies beautifully displayed in corsets and leather. Two cyber punks with neon green hair and kickass T-shirts stood close to the bar and tossed back blood red shots. A trio of gothic Lolitas in pinafores twirled black lace umbrellas and chatted with the drummer and bassist from the band who had opened the night's show.

Among the usual jet-black locks, I spotted blondes, brunettes and redheads. A flash of hot pink caught my eye. The black lace corset and too-short blood-red leather skirt set off a fire within me. Smiling wickedly, I crooked a finger in her direction. Pink's eyes widened, and she practically pranced toward me. Damn, but she was cute.

My gaze drifted back to the two vamps. I beckoned them to join me and Pink. They practically ran to my side. The trio smiled and shook hands. I didn't have to sweet talk them too much. These women knew what they wanted, and they were hell-bent on getting it.

On the way out of the club, I caught Tres dealing with a couple of kids who looked to be underage. The tall, lanky white kid with dyed black hair looked like he was going to piss his pants if Tres kept up his drill sergeant routine. The other kid, the one with impressive dreadlocks, piercings and warm brown skin, didn't seem even the least bit bothered by it. When dreadlocks spotted me in the hallway, he grinned and slapped his friend on the arm.

"What's the problem, Tres?"

"Two underage kids snuck into Slaughterhouse. I caught them snooping around backstage."

Remembering the days when I had done crazy shit like this with Dom, I motioned for the two kids to come closer. "Do you know that I own this place?"

"Yes," they answered in unison.

"Do you know what happens if TABC comes in here and finds underage kids running around?"

Now they both looked down at their feet. "Yes."

I couldn’t blame them for wanting to meet their favorite musicians. Hell, Dom and I had run away from Texas and worked our way to Sweden to find our musical idols. Dom hadn't been much older than these two.

With a sigh, I held out my hand. "Show me what you have for me to sign."

They instantly started buzzing with excitement and whipped out the memorabilia they wanted signed. The kid with dreadlocks offered me a permanent marker, and I made quick work of signing their things. After handing them back, I glanced at Tres. "Get them both shirts. Put them in a cab. Send them home."

"Got it."

I touched the chest of the kid with dreadlocks. "Don't do this shit again. Understand?"

"Yes."

"You wait until you're eighteen to come back here."

"We will."

Certain they would stay away from my club, I nodded at them and slung my arms around the three women. We slowly made our way to the SUV and driver waiting for me out back. The girls wanted to start the party on the drive to the hotel suite, and I couldn't think of a good reason to stop them. By the time we reached the VIP entrance at the rear of the establishment, the girls were panting and my lips were swollen from all the kissing.

But I wasn't even the slightest bit stiff.

Trying not to dwell on the party that *wasn't* starting in my leather pants, I guided the girls into the private elevator and up to the luxury suite on hotel's top floor. My dates wasted no time turning on some music, ordering room service and hitting the bar. I dropped down on a couch and watched them dance for me. It didn't take long for the clothes to start flying.

I had to tear myself away from the enticing sight of the two vamps grinding together on the makeshift dance floor to answer the door and sign for the room service order. While the girls were busy picking through the order, I ducked into the bathroom and dug the extra pill I had tucked into my pocket out of my pants. I tossed it back with a long pull from a vodka bottle and gave my dick a pep talk.

"Come on, you bastard. We have three sexy, wild girls waiting for us out there. Get hard—or else those girls will find a way to get what they want without you."

My pep talk given, I returned to the dining room of the suite. The food play had already started. Pink was smearing whipped cream on the nipples of one of the vamps. I decided to join in the fun. "I think you might be sweeter than my birthday cake..."

But all the nipple sucking and deep French kissing in the world wasn't making me hard. Two blue pills, three hot girls and all that vodka? I should have been relaxed and hard as a bat by now.

If the girls noticed, they didn't say anything. Eventually we were all naked. The party moved into the bedroom—and things took an erotic turn fast. The two dark-haired vamps fell onto the bed with Pink and began attacking her pussy. Soon, they were all thrusting fingers and licking and squealing atop the bed.

Head pounding and heart racing, I stroked my semi-hard shaft with one hand and gripped a tequila bottle in the other. There were men who would give their left nuts to be standing in my spot, but I couldn't get into it. It just wasn't as exciting as it used to be.

Every single fuck had to be more depraved and wilder. It was like a competition to outdo myself. One girl. Two girls. Three girls. Sex toys. Kink. What the hell happened to slow and easy? What happened to simple lovemaking? Why the hell couldn't I find a woman who cared about me? About the real me? About the Step who existed *behind* the lead singer?

Listen to you! You're getting soft, old man.

I was getting soft in more ways than one. My cock wouldn't cooperate, and my frustration level started to rise. I took three long gulps of the tequila I had brought into the bedroom and hissed as it burned its way down my throat. When I lowered the bottle, I noticed I was swaying on my feet. The scene in front of me—the three women writhing with ecstasy—blurred, and I blinked rapidly.

I tried to shake it off, but this wasn't going away. I swallowed anxiously and felt my knees start to shake. *Shit.* Maybe the warning about mixing the dick pills with alcohol was right.

Desperate to sit down, I took one step toward the bed—and fell forward in a dead faint..

CHAPTER TWO

JEMIMA

Rubbing at my tired eyes, I yawned loudly and reached into the refrigerator for a cold soda. I cracked the tab and took a long drink before setting it aside and putting together my brown bag lunch. When I pulled out the plastic container where I stowed deli meat and cheese, I realized we were running low. I hastily calculated the days between now and my next paycheck and closed the box without making a sandwich. Today an extra apple and some peanut butter would have to round out my carrots and whole wheat crackers.

With my lunch packed, I returned to my bedroom and

slipped into the perky pink uniform provided by the five star hotel where I worked as a maid. I pulled on a pair of low cut socks and the ugly but comfortable white shoes I had polished last night before going to bed. I styled my hair into a tightly coiled French twist—one of the three hairstyles permitted within the new strict dress code—and turned to the side to check my reflection.

I slid my hand down the front of the dress and made sure there were no wrinkles in the highly starched outfit. Our housekeeping manager was forgiving, but the new hotel manager was a real hard ass about our appearances. He was the one who had insisted we switch from the more comfortable tunics and slacks to these dresses. Apparently some hotel guests found our old uniforms frumpy and unappealing. Why we needed to look cute and perky to scrub toilets and bathtubs I would never understand!

Glancing at my watch, I snatched up my starched white apron and left my bedroom. I stopped in front of my younger brother's door and rapped my knuckles against it. "Benji? Are you up?" When I heard nothing, I knocked harder. "Benji! Come on, bro. You need to get into the shower and get moving. Benji!"

Bracing myself for the inevitable smell of dirty socks and that nose-wrinkling teenage boy bouquet of hormones and angst that seemed to linger in his room, I opened the door and poked my head inside his room. "Benji? Are you listening to me?"

My gaze landed on his empty bed. A long stream of cuss words left my mouth as I realized he had sneaked out of the house sometime after I had crashed out with exhaustion. Before I could even process how pissed off I truly was, I heard the unmistakable squeal of the back door's hinges. I let the bedroom door slipped closed behind me and strode down the narrow hallway of the single wide mobile home.

When I reached the living room, I caught Benji tiptoeing across the kitchen. He froze at the sight of me. Taking in his nearly all black outfit, I didn't have to guess where he had been. The dark eyeliner smudged under his eyes? The studded leather cuffs circling his wrists? The band tee stamped with the S&M logo? He had been at the Sinister Mayhem show down at Slaughterhouse that I had expressly forbidden him to attend.

Exhaling roughly, I put a hand on my hip and waited for him to speak first. He ran his fingers along one of his dreds and nervously flicked his lip ring with his tongue. "I'm not going to stand here and bullshit you about being sorry, Jem. Because I'm not sorry about going." He flashed that mischievous grin of his. "But I am sorry I got caught."

"This isn't funny, Benji. What if you had gotten into a wreck? Or been injured in a mosh pit? What if you had been arrested for being underage in a Twenty-One-or-Over club?"

"It was Eighteen-and-Up tonight."

"And you're fifteen!"

"Sixteen next week!"

"If you live that long."

"Come on, Jem. Don't be like that."

"Don't!" I shook my head and rubbed my tired face between my hands. Feeling so much older than my twenty-one years, I fought the stressed out tears that pricked at my eyes. "Benji, we are two months into the school year, and the office has already called me three times for your unexcused absences. I get that you think this is some big fucking joke, but the school district is going to slap me with truancy charges and fines. How the hell do you expect me to pay for that?"

Not letting him answer that, I barreled on, "We are in a precarious position here with DFPS. A few more strikes, and they'll take you away from me and toss you in foster care or a group home."

Benji's expression turned serious. He gulped and glanced at his feet. "I'm sorry, Jem."

"Don't be sorry, Benji. Just do better. Okay? You've got to help me out here." I closed the distance between us and grasped his hand. He glanced up at me, and I could see the regret darkening his eyes. I reminded myself that he was still young and dumb and prone to making really boneheaded decisions. "Listen, I love you. You're my brother, and I would do freaking anything for you. *Anything*, Benji. But I need you to meet me halfway, bro."

He surprised me by unexpectedly embracing me.

Crushed in his arms, I realized just how damned big he was getting. He was closing in on six feet, and I could tell where all the groceries were going. He was filling out and turning hard with muscle. Gone was the slightly chubby thirteen-year-old boy I had petitioned and fought the state to gain guardianship over. Here stood a young man on the cusp of adulthood—and I was scared to death I was going to screw him up. I struggled so hard to find the balance of firm disciplinarian to loving sister that he required. I wanted him to be a good man. I wanted him to make something of his life. I wanted Benji to get out of this trailer park and away from the cycle of drugs and violence that had put our mother in prison.

"I didn't mean to upset you like this, Jem. I just—I *really* wanted to go to this show." He released me slowly and stepped back. "I won't do something this stupid again."

I touched his cheek and smiled up at him. "You probably will."

He snorted. "Yeah. Probably."

I flicked the silver hoop dangling from his lip. "Take

that shit out before you go to school, all right? And those too." I pointed at the spider bite piercings on the left side of his mouth and then the barbell in his eyebrow. "You know the school rules." He attended a magnet school for gifted students, and they had a more relaxed policy when it came to their dress code. And thank God! Because he loved pushing the line. "One nose stud and two earrings. That's it, Benji."

"Yeah, I know." His tongue piercing knocked against his teeth. "Principal Nguyen gave me a pass on this one." He flashed the barbell between his lips. "But I won't push it with these."

"Thank you." I shook my head at the mess of makeup on his face. "There are some makeup remover wipes in my bathroom cabinet. You better attack your eyes and cheeks with those first." I picked up his hand again and clicked my teeth at his nail polish. "There's some acetone in that same cabinet. Get those clean." I wrinkled my nose. "And take a shower! You stink of pot and beer and sweat and God only knows what else!"

"I stink of fun!" He reared back and started furiously

grinding on an air guitar. "Man, Jem, you should have seen Leif! He was awesome! And Step? His voice was full-on last night. He's totally recovered from that surgery he had earlier this year."

"I hope you grabbed some video on your phone to keep you amused because your behind isn't leaving this house for two weeks." I waited for him to whine and wheedle, but he showed a bit of my maturity by simply nodding.

"Yeah. Okay, Jem."

"Go on." I gestured toward the back of our trailer. "Get cleaned up and get ready for school. You need to eat before you grab the bus. Don't forget to make your lunch. Pack your inhaler, too."

"I didn't smoke last night. I swear, Jem." He drew a little "X" over his heart. "I'm not stupid enough to put myself back in the hospital."

The last time he had lit up with a couple of friends over the summer, he had ended up in the hospital for three days after an asthma attack from hell. I was still paying off that nightmare and probably would be making payments to the hospital until late next year.

"You light up anything again, and I swear I'm going to pull a Mrs. Rodriguez and go after your behind with a sandal."

The mention of our neighborhood's matriarch and her penchant for whacking bottoms with that thick-soled *chancla* of hers made Benji smile. "I'd like to see you try and catch me."

"I might not be able to catch you, but I bet Mrs. Rodriguez's boys can. Then I'll let her apply that sandal to your backside."

"Fair enough." He said with a laugh and started across the living room. He paused at the small loveseat that was piled high with neatly tied stacks of cleaned, pressed and folded clothing. "Jem! Did you get up early to do these? Because they weren't here when I snuck out last night."

"They had to be done." I didn't mention that we needed the extra cash I earned by doing laundry for the single oilfield workers who lived in our trailer park. His magnet school was free, but all of the activities and trips and school projects he worked on were expensive. Now that our health insurance rates had gone up, our budget was even tighter than normal. Plus Christmas was right around the corner.

"At four in the morning, Jem?" He glanced back at the stacks of clothing. "I'll deliver them when I get home. Friday is early release, and there's no robotics lab today."

"Thank you." It was one less errand I had to tackle when I got home.

"I don't like the way those guys look at you anyway. I'll start doing the drop-offs from now on," he decided.

I didn't argue with him. Frankly, I was relieved. Getting invitations for private turn-down service from skeevy businessmen was bad enough, but having guys who lived down the street trying to pat my ass and making dirty remarks about their underwear was just too much. "They're all labeled. Everyone has paid up except for Jerry down on Twilight Ave. He has a balance on his receipt, but he's good for it."

"I'll take care of it. Do you want me to make dinner?"

"Sure." I glanced at my watch again and grabbed my sack lunch. "I'm going to try to pick up an extra shift at the hotel."

"Don't be too late," he warned. "We're going to see Mom tomorrow, remember?"

"I remember," I assured him. Visiting our mother up at the Henley State Jail wasn't something I was likely to forget. We tried to get up there to see her once a month, but with Benji's birthday, I had decided to take him twice this month. "Make sure you have a nice outfit. Something the duty warden will approve."

"I will," he promised. "I'll roll some change tonight."

Visitors were allowed to bring rolls of quarters to weekend visitation. Mom and Benji could burn through twenty-five dollars at those vending machines faster than any two people I had ever seen. When we had a little extra, we took it with us and gave it to other families waiting to visit their loved ones. It was hard enough for Benji to see Mom locked up in the pen. I couldn't imagine what it was like for the really little kids who had to be searched and swiped with metal detector wands before visiting their mamas. Sometimes a cold soda and a candy bar meant more than just a sugar rush.

Lunch and apron in hand, I swiped my purse from the cheap bookcase near the front door. "Be good today, Benji."

"I will."

"Try to stay awake in class."

"I will."

"Come straight home after class."

"I will, Jem." Exasperation filled his voice. "Will you just go to work already?"

To really rile him up, I leaned over and pecked his cheek. He reacted with the expected disgust. "Man, Jem! That's gross."

Laughing, I left the house and carefully descended the rickety front steps. The sun was just starting to rise and turn the horizon a soft pink. Across the street, I spotted Shay Sandoval pulling into her driveway. Like me, she worked ridiculous hours and too many jobs. Unlike me, she had managed to stay in college. Right now, she was part of a cleaning crew that tackled businesses after-hours and also waitressed third shift at a diner near some of the oil refineries. How she had the energy to do it all perplexed me.

The roar of a motorcycle drew my attention. I recognized the rider as Spider, the man who owned the trailer park. He was also the VP for the Calaveras outlaw motorcycle club and not a man I ever wanted to cross. Of course, he had only ever been kind to me.

So, when he pulled up in front of our house and motioned for me to come talk to him, I didn't dally. "Morning, Spider."

"Good morning, Jem. How's Benji?"

"He's good."

"He's staying out of trouble?"

"Mostly."

Spider laughed. "He's a teenager. That's probably the best you can hope for."

"I think you're probably right."

He toyed with his helmet strap. "Listen, I don't want to keep you. I know you've got to get to work."

"I do."

"I heard that Jackie is back in town."

I blinked at that piece of news. Benji's father and my

stepfather had skipped town not long after our mother had gone to prison.

"He's in trouble, Jem."

"What kind of trouble?"

"He robbed a house where they were cooking some meth. I guess he stole a bunch of product. Needless to say, he's on a lot of shit lists today."

"Great."

"You two need to be careful, okay? I doubt anyone is stupid enough to try to make a move on my property, but you never know with these crack heads and tweakers."

"We'll be careful." I smiled at him. "Thank you for the heads-up."

"If you need anything…"

"I know where to find you." I stepped back and watched him ride away from the house before sliding behind the wheel of my vehicle. I hastily typed out a text to Benji, telling him the details about his bio-dad and urging him to be careful.

B: *We'll be fine. Jackie isn't going to come anywhere near us.*

It wasn't Jackie that had me worried.

Seated behind the wheel of my rundown minivan, I prayed the damn thing would start and not act crazy every time I accelerated or the gears shifted. I needed to get it into the shop but that meant I had to have the money to pay for a mechanic and parts. *Please start. Just get me to work. Please.*

The old beast started up without a fuss, and I relaxed in the lumpy seat. I had bought the minivan on one of those fly-by-night car lots. It was closing in on two hundred thousand miles, and I didn't know how many more it could handle.

Because the air conditioner was shot in the car, I rolled down the windows as I pulled out of the driveway. Fall hadn't brought much of a reprieve from the heat, and this warm, muggy October morning was no different. I peeked at the lightening skyline as I drove away from the park and worried my lower lip. The higher the sun climbed, the more storm clouds I could see. I reached over and switched on the radio. It took a few twists of the knob to find a station giving a weather report.

"...hot and muggy today. Tropical Storm Leo made

that slight left turn we had been expecting and the forecast track has shifted. We're showing a direct hit from this storm and expect landfall late Sunday afternoon. This storm has the potential to produce high, damaging winds and flash flooding..."

I grimaced and turned the radio to my favorite channel. I needed the upbeat pop music to get me through the construction traffic on I-45. As I crawled along the interstate, I ran through my mental checklist for the coming storm. We had been spared hurricanes and big storms the last few years, but it seemed that luck was about to change.

I shuddered at the memories of Tropical Storm Allison. We had lived in a different mobile home then, a really nice double wide in a different area of Houston, but Allison's storm waters had flooded and uprooted it. Mom and Jackie had been high out of their minds at a friend's house when the storm hit. Benji and I had nearly drowned.

That had been the first time DFPS was all up in our business. Not long after our parents got us out of foster care, we had done a series of midnight moves and ended up in progressively worse rent houses and apartments. Mom and Jackie had gotten dragged into the local meth trade—and—well…

But I really didn't want to think about any of *that* right now.

Already tired and so hungry, I pulled into my usual parking spot in the employee lot and headed into the hotel. After clocking in, dropping off my purse and lunch in my locker and tying my apron at the small of my back, I made my way into the employee dining room for our free continental breakfast and morning meeting. I grabbed some bacon, cold cereal, milk and a banana and went to the back table where my friends congregated.

Raucous laughter and hastily spoken Spanish fired back and forth across the table. I was welcomed with smiles and a gentle, fatherly pat on the back from Miguel, a maintenance supervisor. I tucked into my breakfast and listened to the chit-chat. Even though neither of my parents were Latino, I spoke Spanish like a natural and was soon talking to Lupe about her son who went to the same magnet school as Benji.

"*Oye*, Jem, did they tell you about the goth strippers last night?" Diego, one of the security guys who was close to my age, dropped down in the empty seat next to me and poked a straw through the foil lid on his small carton of orange juice.

"No." I finished off the last of my cereal and started peeling my banana. "What happened?"

Diego kicked back in his chair. "So I'm doing my rounds last night. It's late. You know, like, two in the morning. I'm doing my usual hooker check, right? Bouncing those girls who snuck by the front desk," he said and sipped his juice. "I'm up on sixteen dealing with a noise complaint when I get a call on my radio from Jake that there are some vampire hookers going crazy in the pool."

"Vampire hookers?" It sounded like the name of a bad straight-to-DVD movie.

"Crazy, huh?" He laughed. "So I have to see this shit with my own two eyes, right? I get down there—and no joke. These ladies are in their *chonies* in the pool. I mean—

red thongs and black bras and tattoos."

As many years as I had worked at the hotel, I didn't have a hard time imagining that scene. "Were they drunk?"

"You kidding me? They were sweating tequila. They had broken into the pool bar and were raiding the cabinets for liquor. It was straight-up *Girls Gone Wild* down there!"

"So what did you do?"

"I helped Jake get them back into their clothes and into cabs. One of them went all Dracula on me and bit me!"

"What? No way!"

"Look." He pulled down his collar and showed me the nasty bite.

"Did you get that treated?"

He nodded. "I went to the ER and they gave me some antibiotics and sent me back to work. I'm on a double, and I need the hours so I didn't argue."

I understood that only too well. "Where did those women come from?"

"Hell if I know," he said with a shrug. "They probably came in the VIP entrance with one of the biggies upstairs. I'm letting the day shift sort that mess out."

Before I could ask more questions, Richard, the hotel manager, came into the canteen area to make some quick announcements. I didn't miss the sight of Amanda, one of the newer maids who had joined us from a rival upscale downtown hotel, following a few steps behind him. Diego elbowed me and lifted his chin their direction as if to confirm the rumors about the pair.

Richard rudely quieted us in that grating way he had and then explained the hotel's plans for the storm and the changes to some of the upcoming weekend functions. When he was done, we scattered from the employee lounge and got to work.

I joined my fellow maids in our supply room-slash-headquarters and waited for my floor assignments. Juanita, our supervisor, gave out our rooms while she stood in front of the whiteboard and jotted down the number of guests in the hotel this morning and the number of checkouts. We weren't at full capacity but we were dang close. More than half of the rooms were checkouts that needed to be flipped and ready for new guests by three.

It was going to be a long effing day.

"Jemima?"

"Yes, ma'am?" I adjusted my lanyard and carefully crossed the bustling room. With their assignments in hand, my fellow maids were hurrying to get up to their floors and get started on their rooms.

Juanita, a motherly older woman who hailed from Honduras, smiled down at me. "I want you to take Presidential-North, Presidential-South and the Ambassador suite this morning. As soon as you're finished with those three, go down to ten and clean as many rooms as you can before your shift ends. If you want some extra hours, I need help on the second shift, probably down on five, seven and nine."

"I'm on it." I didn't hesitate. The mega-luxury suites took three times as long to clean as the smaller rooms, but there were always big, fat tips. The chance at a second shift was exactly what I needed. Something told me

Juanita was fully aware of my precarious money situation. Maybe I could finally get the van into the shop.

"Wait a second!" Amanda butted into the conversation. "Why is *she* getting three suites? What about the rest of us?"

Juanita cocked her head to the side and gave Amanda a withering stare. "Jemima gets three suites because I know I can count on her to get them done and get them done right. She's been with this hotel for three years, and I trust her work." Juanita took a step forward. "She gave up her chance at the suites last month to help out another maid who needed the hours and the tips. Now it's her turn to get some of that good karma back. *Me entiendes*?"

Amanda didn't answer. She haughtily turned on her heel and headed for the employee elevators. I watched her leave, a knot forming in the pit of my stomach. I had heard a few unsavory things about her from other maids who used to work with her at the other hotel. I hadn't missed the way she took every chance possible to ingratiate herself with Richard, the hotel manager. My internal radar went crazy. That girl was going to be serious trouble for me.

"Don't worry about her," Juanita said. "She'll learn her place here, or she can hit the unemployment line. Now, listen. You've got a banker in from Hong Kong in the south suite, and some big-time rock star in the north. Take the rock star's room first. Those guys are such pigs. They always trash the rooms." She shook her head with disgust. "Go on. Get moving."

"Yes, ma'am." I made my way upstairs to the top floor and into the locked and cleverly concealed supply closet where I stocked a cart with all the cleaning supplies, toiletries, linens and towels I would need to tackle the first suite. Before pushing my cart into the hallway, I scanned my ID card on the digital reader connected to the small screen attached to the cart.

Our supervisors and managers were able to keep track of us using the high-tech system. By logging the preferences of frequent guests into the system, we were better able to anticipate their needs on subsequent visits. This morning, I would log in all sorts of useful information like the number of towels used, the snacks and drinks consumed and whether the guest had used a firm or soft pillow.

I glanced at the screen and read the name of the guest in the presidential suite. *S. Vasiliev.* It didn't sound like the name of a rock star, but a lot of VIPs checked in under their legal names or under the names of their managers to avoid paparazzi or crazed fans. For all I knew, S. Vasiliev was this guy's accountant.

Standing outside the door, I rang the doorbell and waited for an answer. I rang again and nothing. Using my keycard to unlock the door, I knocked on it as I opened it a few inches and poked my head inside. Instantly, I heard the low thump of music coming from the bedroom at the rear of the suite. "Hello? Mr. Vasiliev? This is housekeeping. May I come inside?"

I pushed the door open a few more inches and stepped into the entryway. My gaze flitted around the parlor, and my heart sank. Trashed was an understatement. There were liquor bottles, soda cans and glasses on every flat surface I could see. A red vase had been broken. Glass shards, flowers and water left a mess on the travertine tile. The drapes on the other side of the parlor had been ripped down, and the door that led out to the balcony overlooking downtown Houston was wide open.

Certain the rest of the two-bedroom suite was in even worse shape, I lifted my voice and called out, "Mr. Vasiliev? Sir? This is housekeeping."

Again there was no answer. Cautious and expecting a drunken rock star to come staggering out of the master bedroom at any moment, I carefully crept into the suite. When I got a better view of the dining room, I wanted to cry. It looked like a food fight had taken place in there. Whipped cream dripped down the walls. Raspberries and blueberries had been smashed on the floor. Half a steak was sitting on a chair. Sweet potato fries were all over the counter.

What. The. Fuck.

I couldn't understand these people. Did they think it was funny to leave a mess like this? No, it was even worse than that. To most hotel guests, the maids and support staff were invisible. We existed to serve. We weren't supposed to have feelings. We didn't matter. We were just minimum wage losers.

"Mr. Vasiliev?" I left the dining room and headed toward the master bedroom. The music playing on the other side of the door was loud and heavy on the bass. I segued to the balcony and shut the French doors. I spotted the burned out stubs of blunts littering the ground and railing.

"Really?" I muttered angrily. Rolling my eyes, I walked toward the master bedroom and knocked on the door. "Mr. Vasiliev? Sir? This is housekeeping. Would you like me to clean the room now or come back later?"

Company protocol said I could go ahead and open the door, but I hesitated. I didn't like invading personal spaces, and I really, really didn't want a run-in with an angry, hungover rocker.

But there was something off about this situation. I could feel it in the pit of my stomach. This whole scene had a weird feeling to it. I suddenly remembered what Diego had said about the vampire girls down at the pool. Had their wild night started here?

Imagining the very worst, I knocked twice and twisted the handle. The moment the door opened, I caught a whiff of something terrible. *Oh, God. Don't let him be dead.*

Gulping anxiously, I pushed the door all the way open and stepped into the room. The music in here, something electronic and moody, thumped even more loudly. I quickly spotted the biggest man I had ever seen in my entire life face-down near the bed. He was bare-ass naked and had tattoos covering every inch of skin I could see.

A bottle of tequila had fallen on its side next to his head. All of that expensive top-shelf liquor had spilled out onto the floor and mixed with a pool of vomit. Bloody streaks floated in the tequila. Whether he had cut himself on the glass or in the fall, I couldn't tell.

"Oh my God! Mr. Vasiliev!" I ran across the room and dropped down next to him. "Sir?"

I put a shaking hand on his neck and felt for a pulse. His skin was warm but sweaty. I detected the strong beat of his pulse and breathed a little easier. "Sir? Mr. Vasiliev? Are you okay?"

A low, growling noise rumbled out of his throat. He

started to move but groaned with pain and held still. A massive hand with tattooed knuckles and callused fingers slapped at my hip. He grumbled something in a language I didn't understand. It sounded like Russian. The hotel encouraged us to learn as many greetings as possible in different languages, but I didn't think telling him good morning was going to help much.

"Mr. Vasiliev? Sir? I think we need to call an ambulance."

He grumbled again and yanked on my hip, almost as if he was trying to get me to snuggle in close to him. Eyes wide, I fell to the side and ended up on my bottom. A moment later, he shocked me by lifting his head and dropping it right on my lap. He wrapped both arms around my waist and nuzzled into my belly. He murmured something else in a low, dark voice, his tongue rolling over the Russian syllables, and then began to pet my lower back.

One of his hands moved to my thigh and snaked under my skirt. Shocked by the feel of his hot fingers gliding along my bare skin, I didn't react immediately. It wasn't until he started to move closer to my panties that I flipped out and tried to get free.

But he was so strong! The arm curved around my waist dragged me in tighter and those big fingers of his gripped my inner thigh. A spark of something inappropriate snapped in my lower belly. Ashamed of my response to his manhandling, I grabbed his shoulders and gave him a little shake. "Sir! You need to wake up!"

And stop trying to molest me in your sleep!

That seemed to finally get his attention. His head popped up, and he blinked up at me with confusion. One eye closed and the other narrowed as he tried to focus on my face. He had the greenest eyes I had ever seen. All that smeared stage makeup and blood hid a face that I was certain would be handsome in a rugged sort of way.

As if startled by what he had discovered, he reared back and shook his head. His steadier gaze settled on my face, and he gruffly demanded, "Who the fuck are you?"

I was wrong. There was nothing handsome under that stage makeup. This guy was a Grade-A asshole.

CHAPTER THREE

STEP

Blyad.

Fuck.

Head pounding and body aching, I glanced around the destroyed bedroom of the penthouse suite and cringed. *What the fuck have I done now?*

Snatches of memories flashed before me. The concert. A hug from Hadley. Soaking myself in vodka. The birthday cake. The tequila. All that hot Goth pussy. My pathetic, stupid dick. The pills. The tequila. The floor.

Shit. *Shit.*

Too late, I realized what I was doing to this poor girl.

I had an arm wrapped around her waist and my filthy head in her lap. And my hand? *Fuck*. My hand was on her soft thigh, just inches away from her panties. When I shifted my weight and tried to push up on the hand that had fallen away from her back, I slipped forward and my fingertips brushed her underwear.

Fuck. Cotton, of course. Simple. Sweet. Just like her. One look at those warm brown eyes and full pink lips and dark hair, and I pegged her as the innocent type. This girl hadn't spent much time bruising up her knees to suck rock star cock. She probably hadn't ever slapped at the walls of a bathroom stall as she came hard and loud backstage at a show.

Nyet. Judging by the bright red flush creeping along her neck and into her cheeks, this girl was horrified to have me pawing all over her. Not that I blamed her, of course. Jesus, I must have seemed like a total pig to her.

But that bastard inside me whispered hotly about how much he'd love to corrupt a sweet, young thing like her. I suspected there was a sex kitten just scratching to be set free beneath that innocent exterior.

Not that I would ever find out.

"Sorry, sweetheart," I grumbled and shoved into a kneeling position next to her. My head throbbed violently, and I tried not to lose the last of the tequila swirling around in the pit of my stomach. A soft, cool hand touched my cheek. Startled by her touch, I flinched but didn't move away. Her gentle fingertips prodded a sore spot on my temple. I hissed, and she made an apologetic face.

"Sorry, but you have a nasty cut right here." She bit that pouty lower lip of hers, and I found myself wanting to replace her teeth with mine. "I don't think it needs stitches, but I really think you should see a doctor."

"No doctor," I gruffly replied and pushed her hand away from my face. "I'll be fine."

"I don't know, Mr. Vasiliev. You must have hit the floor pretty hard to knock yourself out."

"Step," I corrected her. "Everybody calls me Step."

"Wait. Are you—?" She tilted her head and studied my face. Her mouth dropped. "You cut your hair! That's why I didn't recognize you. You're Step from S&M."

I didn't know whether to be annoyed or impressed that she had figured out my identity. "You listen to a lot of doom metal, baby girl?"

She snorted. "Not by choice, I assure you."

The remark made something primal in me clench with jealousy. "Your boyfriend a fan?"

"No, my little brother." She slowly stood up, shut off the music and walked into the bathroom. She returned with a towel over one shoulder and then extended her small hands. I realized she wanted to help me stand and almost laughed. She was a tiny little thing with thick curves and a plump ass, but there was no way she had the strength to haul me to my feet.

Even so, I found myself slapping my hand against hers. I shoved off the ground and managed to get into an upright position. I swayed precariously, and she instantly put a hand on my stomach and braced my chest with her shoulder. My head dipped as the world spun around me, and I inhaled the fresh, clean scent of her hair. Was that coconut?

Unable to help myself, I leaned down and breathed in

her smell as she quickly tied the towel around my waist. *Fuck*. If her hair smelled that good, what about the rest of her? A vision of this shy girl on the bed, her maid uniform shoved up around her waist and my face buried between her thighs tormented me. I bet she tasted as sweet as she smelled.

An unexpected throb started in my groin. My dick pulsed to life beneath the towel. For a moment, I couldn't believe what was happening. All those months of fighting with my cock and now this? I swallowed hard and cursed my bad luck. Like this woman wanted anything to do with me! I was a broken, pathetic, passed out drunk.

"Come on," she urged gently. "Let's get you into the shower."

Her kindness unsettled me so I reacted with humor. "You planning on joining me?"

She laughed. "Not a chance."

"You sure? Don't you guys promise a five-star experience?"

"You have ten fingers and two hands." She pushed open the bathroom door. "I'm sure you can create your own five-star experience."

That brought a chuckle out of me. "Funny, sweetheart."

"Lean against the counter," she ordered, and I got the feeling she had done this sort of thing for someone much too often. Not hotel guests, though. She had the practiced movements of a young woman who had been helping an alcoholic or addict parent. I watched her unwrap the provided toiletries and start the shower. "Brush your teeth. It will help you feel better. I'll be back with some first aid supplies and water. You need to hydrate."

I found myself nodding silently and doing exactly as instructed. The first glimpse of my reflection in the mirror, and I winced. My stage makeup had smeared down my cheeks and across my forehead. I turned to the side and examined the cut on my head. It wasn't very deep or too long, but it must have been a bleeder if the amount of dried blood flaking in my short hair was any indication.

I brushed my teeth twice and rinsed three times with

mouthwash to get the awful taste of my debauched night off my tongue. Hands on the counter, I stared at my reflection and experienced the most intense wave of shame and regret. Thirty years old, and I was acting like a goddamned teenager!

You could have died last night, asshole. You could have been robbed or killed or worse. You could have hurt someone.

Instead of the best birthday ever, I had had the worst and most embarrassing one. As I stumbled toward the toilet to relieve my aching bladder, I had a sinking feeling in my stomach. I could just imagine the stories those three chicks were circulating about my limp dick and the nose-dive I'd taken onto the bedroom floor. The fact that they hadn't stuck around to make sure I was alive hurt in a way I would never admit to anyone. To know that they hadn't even cared about whether or not they had left a corpse on the bedroom floor wasn't a good feeling.

"Mr. Vasiliev? Sir?" She knocked on the door. "Are you decent?"

I laughed harshly. "Hardly, sweetness."

"You know what I mean."

"Yes."

She entered the bathroom and placed a small first aid kit on the counter along with bottles of sports drink and water. "When you're finished showering, I'll help you bandage your cut." She glanced back toward the bedroom. "Where are you clothes?"

I scratched at the heavy, raspy shadow of a beard on my chin. "I think I lost my shirt somewhere in the living room and my pants in the dining room."

She dropped her gaze. "Oh. Well. I'll go get them for you."

"You don't have to do that." I didn't know why, but the idea of her hunting down my clothes and finding the evidence of all the crazy shit I had been up to made me feel really bad.

She shrugged. "It's my job."

Guilt crashed onto my shoulders like an anvil dropped from the top of a high-rise. I thought of the absolute mess we had made of the suite. This one girl had to clean it all up. How many other maids had I tormented and fucked over with my bad behavior? Shit, I was not proud of that at all. One more check for the rotten bastard column.

Not liking myself very much, I unwrapped the towel and stepped into the walk-in shower. The blast of steam and heat sent a wave of unexpected dizziness through me, and I leaned to the left. In an instant, she was there. She swooped in under my arm and caught me around the waist. I found my balance and staggered back under the spray of hot water, dragging her with me.

She squealed and tried to disentangle herself as the water soaked right through her uniform. That sound she made sent a shockwave of want and need straight down to my cock. Her lush breasts pressed against my body, and I wanted to cup them in my hands, to feel the weight of all that soft flesh on my bare palms.

She wiggled to get free and my arms instinctively tightened around her. She gazed up at me with confusion. Little beads of water rode her jawline and the bridge of her nose. I didn't know what it was about this girl but that one simple look had ensnared me. She was like a damned siren, and I wanted to hear her sing.

I captured her mouth before she could protest. Her hands flew to my chest, first to push me away, but then I stabbed my tongue between her lips and she whimpered. Her fingers curled against my pecs and then her hands slid to my biceps. She held on tight as I cupped the back of her head and plundered her mouth.

I battled the urge to pick her up, shove her thighs apart and sink into her soft, slick pink. I managed to ease off the throttle and slow my sensual attack. She gulped and panted against my chest, her face just inches above my navel. This close, I was reminded of how short she was. An uncomfortable thought hit me. "How old are you?"

"Twenty-one."

I breathed easier knowing the age difference wasn't as big as I had feared.

"Why?"

I cupped her face and bent down. "Because now

I don't have to worry about doing this again."

This time she didn't fight my kiss. She melted into me and let me have my way—but not for too long. Just when the kiss was starting to get really interesting, she tugged free and shook her head. "We have to stop."

"Why?" My voice was thick with desire.

"Because I'm getting all wet."

I laughed darkly. "Baby, that's the idea."

Her face turned bright red, and I almost felt bad about teasing her. Almost. "Sorry, sweetheart."

"Jem," she said. "My name is Jem."

"Jem." I liked the sound of that. "Short for?"

"Jemima."

I smiled and bent down to kiss her again. "Come here, Jemima Puddleduck." I didn't think it was possible, but she turned even redder at my joke about the children's book. "What is it?"

"That's, um, actually what inspired my mom to

name me Jemima," she admitted a bit bashfully. "My little brother is Benjamin."

I couldn't decide if naming two kids after Beatrix Potter characters was the sweetest thing I had ever heard or the weirdest. "That's...interesting."

She laughed and rolled her eyes before playfully shoving me away from her. "Interesting is a good way to describe my family."

I wanted to grab her and drag her right back into the shower, but I let her go. When she hid behind the door, she unknowingly touched off a primitive chase response. Like a wolf who had caught the scent of a deer, I wasn't about to stop chasing now. I could still see her reflection in the mirror, but she didn't know that.

While I soaped up, I watched her peel out of the pink uniform dress. She wore simple pink panties and a white bra. After having sexually confident and scantily clad women throwing themselves at me and chasing their fantasies of being fucked by a rock star, it was strange to see a woman behaving so modestly and wearing something so plain. All these years, I had thought that I wanted a woman who could match or beat me in the bedroom department, but maybe I had been wrong. Considering the way my body was responding to Jem, I seemed to have swung to the opposite end of the spectrum. There was something alluring about shy, kind Jemima the Maid.

She wrung out the excess water from her dress into the sink and then ducked behind the door again. I watched her blast the damp fabric with the hair dryer. When I stepped out of the shower, I grabbed a clean towel, dabbed at my wet skin and wrapped it around my waist. I snatched the plush robe from the back of the door and thrust it at her. "Wear this."

She shot me a grateful look, and I realized that she wouldn't have taken the robe if I hadn't offered it to her. She would have stood there, soaking wet in her undies, rather than break some inane rule about using the hotel's guest amenities. I shook out the robe and draped it around her shoulders. Even though I really wanted to see her naked, I decided not to push her, not yet. I turned my back. "I won't peek."

"Thank you." Her voice seemed smaller now and uncertain.

Fast and rushed was my speed, but I got the feeling Jem liked to take things slow and easy. Not wanting her to pull away from me now, I hurried to reassure her about what had just happened. "I plan to kiss you again today and take you to dinner and then kiss you again."

"Oh." She seemed surprised. "I thought maybe..."

"Maybe I drag all hotel maids into the shower with me and kiss them like that?"

"Well…"

"I get around, sweetheart, but I'm not that bad." I glanced over my shoulder to find her hugging the robe tightly to her chest and staring at me as if she couldn't quite figure me out. There was something about her that had grabbed hold of me and wouldn't let go.

I was suddenly dragged back to my childhood, to a late night when my dad had drunkenly told me about the day he had met my mother. *Like a lightning bolt to the head.* That's how he had described it. I hadn't understood it then, but I sure as hell did now. All these years of looking all around the world for the woman who would shake me up and make my heart race—and she had been right here in Houston the entire time!

"I'm flattered, Mr. Vas—Step, but I can't have dinner with you." She draped her damp panties and bra on the towel bar.

A flutter of panic invaded my chest. "You have a boyfriend?"

"No."

I glanced at her left hand. "A husband?"

She let loose an amused laugh. "No."

"So what's the problem?"

"I'm working a double shift today."

I started to say that wasn't a problem, that we could just go out later, but then I realized how tired she would be after sixteen hours of backbreaking work scrubbing floors, cleaning bathrooms and making beds. "I'll take you out for breakfast tomorrow."

She shook her head. "Sorry. I have plans."

Now I was getting frustrated. "Cancel them."

"They can't be canceled."

I let out an irritated huff. "I want to see you. Properly," I added. "I want to take you out."

"I want you to take me out." Her eyes widened

slightly, and I could tell she hadn't meant to admit that. I wanted to smirk triumphantly but didn't. "Look," she said with a little sigh, "my family life is really complicated. That kiss in the shower? It was fun, but it can't happen again."

"Says who?"

"Says me."

"Why?"

"Step, you don't want to get involved in my crazy, hot mess of a life. We're not compatible. Let's just chalk up that kiss to your hangover and let it go."

"No." I strode toward her and boxed her in with my larger body. I planted my hands on the wall just above her head and bent down until we were nearly eye to eye. She licked her lips and stared up at me with apprehension. "I'm not going to hurt you."

"I know."

"So why are you looking at me like that?"

"Because I think you're going to get me into

trouble," she admitted quietly.

I couldn't help but smile at that. "I have no doubt."

"Step…"

"Jem," I cut in before she could come up with a million reasons why this wouldn't work. "I'm asking for one date. Say yes."

"I…"

I nuzzled her neck and nipped at her jaw before teasing my mouth against hers. "Say yes."

"Yes." Her breathy answer made my balls ache. I wanted to hear her whispering yes like that when she was pinned beneath me on a bed. "One date."

"Tomorrow," I decided. "I'll pick you up."

"Not too early," she said. "Benji and I have to drive up to Dayton in the morning to visit our mom. It will probably be an all-day thing."

"You and your brother live together?" It didn't surprise me. She struck me as the kind of woman who took care of her own. Hell, she had just dragged me out of my tequila-and-Viagra-induced coma into the shower. If she would do that for a stranger, I could only imagine the lengths she would go to when it came to protecting and caring for her family.

I liked her more and more.

"Yes, we live together. He's still in high school."

That didn't quite make sense to me. "Your mother is back home in Dayton while you two are here in Houston?"

She hesitated before reluctantly admitting, "Mom is locked up in Henley doing a twenty year bid."

Twenty years? Jesus Christ! What had that woman done?

As if reading my mind, Jem explained, "She was picked up during a drug raid at our old house where they were cooking meth. My little brother was in the house so she got hit with a list of charges a mile long."

"I'm sorry." I didn't know if that was the right thing to say, but I wasn't sure what else was appropriate.

"Don't be. She got what she deserved for putting him at risk like that. She did stupid, selfish things that hurt us, and now she's paying the price."

She didn't speak with malice or anger in her voice. I heard only resignation. "What about your father? He let her keep your brother in a house like that?"

"My father is dead. Benji's dad was locked up in the county jail on a DUI charge. By the time he got out, I had custody of Benji, and he split."

I decided not touch the stepdad in county lockup part. "Custody? How old is your brother?"

"He'll be sixteen in a few days. I took custody of him almost three years ago."

I hastily did the math and found myself in awe of her. How many other eighteen-year-olds would have gone to that trouble to save a younger sibling from foster care? What else had she given up to take on the role of parent at eighteen? College? Her dreams?

I thought of how selfish I had been at that age and the stupid shit I had gotten tangled up in at an even earlier age. Semyon, my older brother, had saved my ass on more than one occasion. He had gotten me through high school graduation before giving me the speech about being a man and making a life for myself. He had chosen to join the Navy, and I had chosen to run away to Los Angeles with Dom. Eventually, we had ended up in Oslo, of all the cold fucking places, and bumped into Tor and Leif. The rest was metal history.

"Like I said," she whispered, "my family is a hot mess of crazy."

I realized she had misinterpreted my silence as disapproval. I brushed my knuckles down her cheek. "You're a good person. You love your brother.

That's all that matters."

"To you, maybe." She dropped her gaze, and my damned chest ached, my heart slamming into my ribcage at the realization that she had spent so many years having people look down on her for family's bad choices that she automatically expected everyone to call her trash or worse.

I slid my fingers under her chin and tipped her head back, forcing her to meet my gaze. "Right now, my opinion is the only one that matters. You've shown me that you're a good person, Jemima. I believe what people show me."

Not wanting her to feel badly about anything she had just told me, I confessed, "When I was a kid, I used to run pickups for an Albanian bookie. I got it into my head that I could start running my own book on the side. Let's just say that didn't go over well, and I damn near got clipped one night. If it hadn't been for my brother and Ten, my cousin, I would have ended up in a cement foundation or tossed off a boat somewhere off the coast of Galveston."

"When I was a little girl, my dad got into some trouble with the cartel. He took something he shouldn't have." She drew a slow finger across her throat. "No one was ever arrested for it, but we knew."

"I'm sorry, Jem." I couldn't even imagine the horrors she had probably witnessed as a child. The urge to protect her flared hot and steady. I wanted to wrap her up in my arms and run away with her, take her back to my apartment and keep her safe there.

Too fast. You're moving too fast. Get a grip. You just met this girl.

But as I gazed down at her, I knew. I fucking *knew* that she was the one.

Fifty years from now, I was going to tell our grandkids about the day I had embarrassed myself in front of their grandmother by letting her find me passed out drunk in a trashed hotel room—and the way she had treated me kindly. I would tell them that was the moment I had decided she was the one I had been waiting for all these years.

So fuck it. Fast and hard had always served me well.

Today? I was going after Jemima—and nothing would stop me.

CHAPTER FOUR

JEM

Weirdest. Day. Ever.

I glanced to my left and couldn't believe that Step was down on his hands and knees scrubbing the dirty dining room floor with a microfiber cloth. When I had tried to clean up the mess in the bedroom, he had flipped out and ordered me into the parlor area to tackle the mess in there. At first, I had been bewildered by his reaction, but then I had recognized the shame darkening his green eyes.

Cleaning the suite in a bathrobe had felt weird at first, but the work had to be done so I had learned to deal with it. Not that Step fit the part of housekeeper any better! He looked utterly ridiculous rocking black leather pants while he attacked that stain and yet somehow also intensely sexy.

As if sensing my stare, he glanced at me and flashed a sinful smile. Feeling suddenly embarrassed, I turned my attention to the dining table I was resetting with replacement china from the supply cupboard. I could feel the heat rising in my cheeks and a throbbing pulse centered between my thighs. I had been kissed plenty of times in my twenty-one years but that kiss in the shower? That one single kiss had obliterated every other kiss from my memory.

I couldn't even imagine what he was like in bed. If one kiss made my knees knock together and my stomach wobble, sex would probably kill me. My sexual experience was meager compared to his. One boyfriend and two attempts at sex had been enough for me to swear it off. Then I had taken custody of Benji and all hopes for a social life had been demolished. Trying to raise a teenager while I was a teenager took every single ounce of energy I had.

But as I started pushing a microfiber mop around the vast swaths of marble and hardwood, I found myself craving some real adult interaction. Step's kisses and his touch had relit the passionate fire that had been snuffed out by a hard life and hard work. He made me feel things I didn't know I was capable of feeling.

And yet I couldn't quite trust him.

I had discovered him naked and face-down in a puddle of his own mess after spending the night with a trio of hard-partying girls. Judging by the looks of the suite and the antics Diego had described, those girls had had more fun than Step. I almost felt bad that he had spent his thirtieth birthday passed out on the floor.

Almost.

"What are you thinking about that has you so quiet?" Step used his uncommon height to easily fix the drapes. "Are you rethinking our date?"

"No." From this vantage point, I had the perfect view of his unbelievably hot body. He had outrageously muscled arms and a well-defined chest. My gaze travelled along his tattooed stomach to the dangerous dip in the front of his pants. There was no mistaking the outline of his cock tucked to the left. Panicked visions of that monstrous thing trying to impale me sent a quiver of fear through my belly.

"Good." He adjusted the folds of the fabric and thankfully seemed oblivious to me ogling him. He unlocked the French doors leading out to the balcony and began collecting the trash out there. When he returned with the whole mess of cans and bottles and other refuse in his arms, he shot me a concerned look. "Is it okay for me to toss all of this in the trash?"

I understood what he was asking. "Dude, hiding a handful of burnt out blunts in a garbage bag is probably the *least* worst thing I've had to toss in one these rooms."

He didn't seem to find that amusing. "Some people are dicks." My eyebrows arched, and he looked suddenly chagrined. "Yes, present company included," he amended. Then, more seriously, he said, "Jemima, I wasn't smoking dope last night. I did a lot of stupid things, but I wasn't on drugs."

That was some small consolation. "So that whole mess in there?" I gestured to the master bedroom as he dumped his load of trash into the garbage can attached to my cart. "Are you a binge-drinker?"

"No, I'm just incredibly dumb." He moved around the cart and took the mop out of my hand. "I enjoy a drink now and then, but last night was the first time in years that I've gotten wasted like that." His jaw hardened. "I'm not my father."

That got my attention. "What does that mean?"

"He was an alcoholic."

"Oh. I'm sorry."

He shrugged in a nonchalant way that I instantly recognized as a defensive maneuver. "He was weak."

"He was human," I corrected. "We all make mistakes, Step." I pointed to the bedroom where I had discovered him passed out on the floor. "Even you."

"And you?" He studied me for an unnerving moment. "What was the last mistake you made?"

Not liking the intense turn this discussion had taken, I joked, "Taking this room assignment."

Step stunned me by slipping his arm around my waist and hauling me close. He dipped his head and smiled. "Give me a little more time. I'll change your mind."

His lips were on mine again, and I clutched at his arms. He didn't need more time to change my mind. In fact, I was thanking my lucky stars that Juanita had given me this suite. I didn't know what was happening between us but I liked it. The illicit thrill of what I was doing rocked me to the very core. This wasn't me. I wasn't the girl who did crazy things like this but I couldn't find a single good reason to stop him, not yet.

He took his time loving my mouth, flicking his tongue against mine and then sucking gently on the tip. I would have dropped to the floor if Step hadn't been holding me up. Those powerful arms of his easily supported my body. I shivered when his lips moved along my jawline. He pushed aside the lapels of the robe and skimmed his lips down the curve of my throat.

When he tried to kiss my breast, I gently pushed his head to the side and closed my robe. "No."

He stopped instantly. Though he seemed to be one of

those alpha dominant types who enjoyed running the show, he respected my boundaries. Our gazes clashed as we exchanged heated breaths. "Did I—?"

"I'm at work," I interjected quickly. "We shouldn't be doing this."

I could tell he wasn't thrilled with that answer, but he nodded and stood up straight. "I shouldn't have pushed."

I bravely reached for his hand. "It's just the wrong time."

Step smiled and lifted my fingers for a sweet kiss. "I can wait for the right one."

"Well," I gently tugged my hand free, "you may be waiting a long time. I have two more suites and probably a dozen more rooms to clean before the end of my shifts."

"Jesus, Jem," he said with shock in his voice. "That's a lot of work for one little woman."

I bristled at that remark. "I'm not that little."

"What are you? Five flat?"

"Five-two," I replied. "Thank you very much."

He crossed his arms and laughed. "No wonder my

neck is aching. I'm a full foot and three inches taller than you."

"Well, yeah, because you've got all that Russian DNA running through your veins."

He chuckled. "We aren't all big and tall." He paused. "Well, okay, in my family, we are."

"Do you have a large family here?" I asked as I headed for the bathroom to change back into my hopefully dry uniform.

"No. It's just me and my brother and our cousin." Step followed me into the neat and tidy bedroom but no farther. "We have a lot of friends here. The Russian community is pretty tight."

I slipped behind the door but left it cracked so we could talk. "How old were you when you came to this country?"

"Seven," he said, his voice taking on a faraway quality. "Talk about a culture shock!"

I didn't know enough about Russian politics or history to really understand what that meant. I had a vague idea of what it would have been like. "Did you speak English?"

"Only a very little," he said. "I got lucky and met Dom that first day of school. He was a big, rough bastard even back then. After he laid out the first kid who made fun of me, we were inseparable."

"He sounds like a good friend."

"He's the very best." His voice sounded louder, as if he had moved closer to the door. I glanced at the mirror and caught him peeking at me as I fastened the hooks of my bra. I held my breath when he pushed the door open and stepped into the bathroom. What was he up to now?

Step took down my uniform from the hook on the back of the door and rubbed the fabric between his hands. Satisfied it was dry, he walked toward me and carefully helped me into the dress. His huge hands looked so strange handling the tiny white buttons lining the front, but he showed a tremendous amount of finesse in the way he deftly slipped them into place. He fixed the collar and trailed a finger down my neck. "I wish you could feel how much I want to rip this off of you and throw you down onto the bed we just made."

I gulped at his frank admission.

"Would you like that?" Step slid his hand along the back of my neck and caressed my skin with slow swipes of his thumb.

"Yes," I admitted softly, "but I sure would hate to have to change those sheets again. Those tucked corners are a bitch to get right on these king size beds."

He chuckled low and rough and then captured my mouth in a long, slow kiss. "You're driving me fucking crazy, *rybka*." He nuzzled our noses together. "You've got me cleaning floors and making beds and fixing drapes—and I don't think I've ever enjoyed spending this much time with a woman."

I smiled up at him. "We've set the bar pretty low for our first date."

"You're right. I'll cancel my plans to take you to Samovar. We'll hit up a drive-thru on the way to a round of miniature golf."

He was teasing me, and I loved it. "You're not the way I thought you would be."

"What do you mean?" His thumb swept along the

curve of my lower lip.

"I've been listening to your songs for years, and I've sort of followed your career through Benji. I had this idea of what type of person you would be. Then I found you on the floor this morning, and you were kind of a jerk to me, and I was sure you were going to be an asshole."

The corner of his mouth lifted. "I deserve that."

"Maybe," I said uncertainly, suddenly doubting my judgment of him. I had no doubt that he had done some really jerky things in his life, but I could see that there was a core of goodness in him. "I'm glad I gave you a chance."

"Give me one more chance tomorrow, and I'll prove that I'm not as awful as my reputation would have you believe." He nipped at my lower lip before kissing me insistently. His big hands glided down my back and cupped my bottom.

A frisson of wild delight coursed through me, and it took every ounce of my willpower to push him away. "I need to go. I'm running behind, and I have a lot of work to get done."

"Do you want me to help you?"

"Are you serious?"

"Yes." He was absolutely sincere in his offer. "It's my fault you're late." He caressed my backside. "I can help you catch up."

"I appreciate the offer, but I can't risk it. My supervisor would write me up, and the hotel manager would have my ass."

"I'll break his arm if he gets anywhere near *my* ass." He gave my bottom a possessive squeeze that sent the most incredibly powerful and confusing thrill right through me. Was I really getting excited by this? The pulsing ache between my thighs confirmed that, yes, I was.

I closed my eyes as Step kissed my cheeks and throat. He kneaded my bottom and then gave it a soft swat. "You better get out of here while you can. I'm about five seconds away from throwing you over my shoulder and carrying you to bed."

I heeded his warning and scurried out of the bathroom. I could hear him moving around the bedroom while I finished packing up my cart. He emerged as I was pushing it toward the front door and trailed close behind. I had only taken three steps into the hall when he suddenly grabbed and spun me around before claiming another kiss, this one heated and frenzied.

I felt his hand tucking something into my pocket as he ended our explosive kiss. When I glanced down, I caught the sight of crisply folded hundred dollar bills and a business card. I grasped his wrist to stop him. "What are you doing?"

"It's your tip."

"Step—"

"No," he said with a shake of his head. "This room was a disaster, and you took care of me." He gestured to his bandaged cut. "I want you to have it."

I wanted to argue with him, but I could tell this was a fight I wouldn't win. Thoughts of the groceries I could buy and the nice birthday gift I could get Benji ran through my head. "Thank you."

He touched my lips with his finger. "You don't need to do that." He kissed my forehead. "The business card has my private number on it. Call me tonight when you get off work."

A soft, disbelieving voice in the back of my head wondered how many other girls had been slipped that phone number. I thought of all the stories I heard around the locker room from some of the maids who let the wealthy businessmen who frequented the hotel enjoy their company. How was this any different?

You're not special. Don't get your hopes up. He'll probably cancel the date once he realizes the mistake he's made.

"Don't do that, Jem." He frowned down at me.

"Do what?"

"I can practically hear your thoughts." He brushed a few wisps of hair that had escaped my twist behind my ear. "You're thinking that I do this with all the hotel maids, but you're wrong. There are only three women who have that private number—and I haven't dated any of them. Two of them are like little sisters to me and the third is like my mother. Do you understand, *rybka*?"

I nodded. "Yes."

"Good." He patted my bottom. "You better go."

"Yes, I really should."

"Call me. Tonight. As soon as you get home," he called after me as I pushed my cart away from his door and toward the south penthouse suite on the opposite end of the floor.

"I will." I waved back at him and then kept moving forward. Still a bit dazed and bewildered by my strange morning with Step, I entered the empty suite and got to work. This set of rooms looked as if it had barely been touched so it didn't take me long to leave it gleaming and squeaky clean. After locking away the cart for that floor, I hopped onto the employee elevator and rode down a couple of floors to the next big suite I had been assigned.

When I stepped off the elevator, I found Richard and Amanda talking quietly near the supply room. I wasn't sure what she was doing on this floor since she had been assigned rooms on the lower floors, but I wasn't about to get involved in her nonsense. I checked out a cart from that floor's closet and stocked it with all the necessary items.

"You're running behind this morning," Richard said as he checked his watch. "Is there a reason for that?"

"One of the suites was in pretty bad shape." There was no reason to lie to him. Maybe I had a thing going with Step and maybe I didn't, but that didn't change the facts. He and his *guests* had caused a significant amount of damage to the hotel's property. There wasn't any way he was getting out of that. "Presidential-North," I clarified.

"Turn in your report before the end of your shift. I need to bill the guest."

"Yes, sir."

Richard stood there for a moment longer. "Is there a reason your hair is damp?"

I reached up and self-consciously touched my hair. "I had an accident while cleaning the shower."

"I see." Richard narrowed his eyes. "Your uniform is wrinkled. You know my policy."

"Yes, sir." I smoothed out the new folds and creases. "I'll make sure that my uniform is perfect when I come to work on Sunday."

He nodded stiffly. "See that it is—or else I'll dock your pay."

"Yes, sir."

"Get back to work."

"Yes, sir." I swallowed nervously and pushed my cart toward the Ambassador suite. I glanced back and discovered the manager studying me intently. Something told me I hadn't seen the last of him today.

CHAPTER FIVE

STEP

I couldn't stop thinking about her. I paced the suite like a caged lion and tormented myself with memories of our kisses. My palms fucking burned with the feeling of her plump ass filling them. I was in absolute hell.

Jemima had demolished the mental block that had prevented me from getting hard. My cock had been stiff for hours, and my balls ached. I needed some relief. I considered going into the bathroom to take the edge off, but I wanted her. I wanted to feel her hands on my shaft. I wanted her warm lips wrapped around my dick and her soft, pink tongue flicking at my cockhead.

Jem. Jem. Jem. I wanted Jem.

A knock at the door interrupted my manic pacing. "Mr. Vasiliev? This is Richard Horton, the general manager of the hotel. May I speak with you for a moment?"

Shit. I should have checked out an hour ago, but the thought of retreating to my lonely penthouse a few blocks over hadn't been very appealing. For one, it was empty. For another, *she* wasn't there.

I crossed the suite and opened the door to find a shorter, slightly pudgy man standing there. He didn't smile at me, and he had a security officer behind him. "Yes?"

"May we come inside, Mr. Vasiliev?"

I stepped aside and waved them into the parlor. "What can I do for you?"

"I'm Richard Horton, the manager, and I think we need to have an uncomfortable conversation, Mr. Vasiliev."

I laughed at that. "Look, if this is about the girls who were with me last night, I'll pay for the damages they caused."

"That wasn't up for negotiation," Richard replied. "Your final bill is already being prepared, and we have papers you'll need to sign that say you won't trespass on the hotel property again."

"Fine." I didn't fault the guy for being a dick about it. He was responsible for the property, after all. "I'm happy to settle up when I checkout."

"And when will that be?"

I glanced at the security officer who looked as if he wanted to be anywhere but here. "Considering you brought the hotel's hired muscle with you, I'm guessing I'll be checking out soon."

"Yes, I think that's best."

"Fine."

Richard stepped forward and sneered at me. "We run a clean hotel here."

I frowned at him. "I'm sure you do."

"Diego?" He addressed the security guard without taking his eyes off of me. "Please escort Mr. Vasiliev down to the lobby and out of the hotel."

"Yes, sir."

Richard strode out of the suite, and I stared after him, trying to figure out what the hell his problem was. The security guard, a much shorter Latino guy, gestured toward the bedroom. "Should I call for bell service?"

"I don't have any bags."

"Then we should get moving." Diego headed for the door. "Because if he gets to Jem before we do—"

"What?" I clapped a hand on the younger man's shoulder and spun him around. "What are you talking about?"

"That dick thinks Jem was in here blowing you for money, man. He's about to go fire her."

"What?" Anger burned through me with the fury of a thousand suns. "Why the fuck would he think—" I stopped as I thought of the way I had kissed her and slipped that tip into her pocket. "*Blyad.*" I scratched my nails against my scalp. "That wasn't what happened. I was tipping her."

"And kissing her," Diego retorted, his mouth slanted with disapproval. "Richard has his nose so far up

Amanda's ass he'll believe anything she tells him, but I've known Jem for years. She isn't like that. I don't know why the hell she was kissing a guy like you, but she isn't one of those *cochinas* who flops on her back for the VIP guests."

"A guy like me? What the fuck is that supposed to mean?"

"Really, dude? I was the one who had to chase your groupies from one fucking end of this hotel to the other last night. I got slapped in the face and bit!" He yanked down the collar of his uniform shirt to show a dark bruise in the shape of teeth. "I know your type. I know what happens to nice girls like Jem when they get involved with pricks like you."

"You don't know shit about me." I stormed for the door. "You can either help me find Jem or I'll tear this hotel up floor by floor until I find her."

Diego raced after me. "She's down on five. Hey! Man! This way. We'll take the employee elevator. It will be faster."

Irritated with the fucked up way a harmless kiss had

spiraled out of control, I joined Diego in the employee elevator. The security guard said nothing as we dropped more than a dozen floors. When we stepped off the elevator, I spotted a maid leaning out a door and listening intently. She had a worried look on her face. A heartbeat later, I understood why.

"That is *not* what happened!" Jem's raised voice came out of a hotel room with a door that had been propped open by a triangular wooden block. A cleaning cart sat in the hallway. "I got wet helping him get cleaned up after I found him sick in his room."

"We have you on camera! You can lie all you'd like, but I know what I saw and I know what I can prove with our security footage."

"And what, exactly, can you prove?"

"Empty your pockets."

"What?"

"Empty. Your. Pockets."

"No!"

"Why not? Are you afraid that I'll see the wad of bills he paid you for sucking his dick? Huh? What's the going rate for Houston hookers these days?"

My heart jumped into my throat, and I saw red. Like a raging bull, I raced down the hall and into the hotel room where Richard had Jem cornered and backed up against a bed. The sight of the bigger, taller man forcing her into a position like that infuriated me. The expression of humiliation on Jem's face at being accused of selling her body was too much for me to handle.

I gripped Richard's shoulder and jerked him around before grabbing two handfuls of his suit jacket and lifting him up off the floor. I slammed him into the wall and got into his face. "Don't you ever talk to her like that again! You so much as frown in her direction, and I'll break your fucking knees."

Eyes wide, Richard sputtered. "You can't—"

"Try me." I gave him a shake. "If you want to accuse someone of doing something illegal, you bring that shit to me. You don't go behind my back and attack her."

"I didn't—"

"The hell you didn't," I snarled. "I don't like bullies, and I really don't fucking like you."

"Step." Jem quietly urged me to let him go by placing her hand on my arm.

Still glaring at Richard, I released my clenched hold on his suit and let him fall to the floor. Diego chose that moment to finally come into the hotel room. Red-faced, Richard shouted, "Get them both out of the hotel. Now!" He pointed a finger at Jem. "You're fired. Get your stuff out of the locker room, turn in your lanyard and get off this property."

Now I really wanted to plant my fist in this fucker's face. First, he had accused Jem of being a whore, and now he was firing her? "You son of a—"

"No." Jem put a hand on my chest, stopping my forward advancement. "He's not worth the trouble."

Her petting hand soothed my raw burst of explosion. She managed to calm me unlike anyone else ever had. I glanced down at the small hand on my chest and clasped it tightly with my fingers. I turned toward the exit and gave her hand a tug. "Let's go."

"Where?" she asked as she hurried to keep up with me.

"Home."

"Home? My house?"

"No." I pulled her into the elevator and smacked the button for the lobby. "Mine."

"Step!" She shouted my name loudly enough that it echoed in the small metal box. "I can't just go home with you."

"Yes, you can."

"No, I can't. I have to start sending out resumes and go home to look over my checking account and figure out whether or not I can file for unemployment or try to get my job back."

The thought of Jem having to work with that asshole again sickened me. "You are not coming back here."

"Whoa." She poked my chest twice. "I appreciate you coming in there to defend me, but you do not get to tell me where I can or cannot work."

Shit. I realized too late what a psycho, possessive jerk I must have sounded like with that decree. "I didn't mean it like that." I still held tight to her hand and rubbed my thumb across her knuckles. "You are too good to come back here and work for someone who would accuse you of something like that."

Her irritated expression softened. "I know."

"But?"

"But I need the money," she said matter-of-factly. "I have bills to pay and medication to buy and—"

"Come work for me."

Fuck. *Fuck*. Did I really just say that? Was I losing my mind?

Yes.

I was losing it for this wildly beautiful young woman who had ensnared me with her sweet smile and gentle touch.

"I can't work for you."

"Yes, you can." I slid my hand to the back of her neck and peered down at her face. "I have a big apartment a few blocks from here. Come be my personal housekeeper." With a bit of a sly smile, I added, "But I get to pick your uniform."

She rolled her eyes and smacked my arm. "Not happening."

I laughed. "Fine. Lady's choice on the uniform. Come work for me. Let me help you out because this is my fault."

"I said you were going to get me into trouble, didn't I?'

"Yes, you did." I kissed her forehead. "I'm sorry, Jem. I didn't mean to crash into your life and ruin everything." I caressed her cheek. "What do you say? Yes?"

She blew out a long, slow breath. "I'll work for you—but just until I get back on my feet."

I had no intention of letting her walk away to another job, but she didn't need to know that. The elevator doors opened, and there were already two security guards waiting for us. One of them had a box that I assumed contained her personal items from her locker. Fucking bastards! Throwing her out like that? I silently cursed myself for not decking Richard when I had the chance.

Taking the box from the security guard, I held her hand and kept my head high as we walked side by side across the opulent hotel lobby and out to the valet station. I remembered that I had taken a private car and turned to Jem. "Do you have a car?"

She gave my hand a tug. "This way."

I trailed her around the side of the hotel, down a side street and onto the open air parking lot where employees parked their vehicles. She led to me a beat-up minivan that probably should have been sold for parts and scrap metal about fifty thousand miles ago. It hardly looked safe to drive. "Give me your keys."

"Why?"

"I'll drive." I didn't want her behind the wheel of this old beast if it decided to die on us.

She fished her keys out of the box I held but didn't relinquish them just yet. "Are you insured?"

I smiled at how careful she was about everything. The guilt weighing down my shoulders grew heavier. I couldn't even imagine what she was feeling after I had just totally fucked up her life by getting her fired. "Yes, and my license is valid. I haven't had so much as a parking ticket in six or seven years."

"All right." She handed over the keys, and we stowed her box in one of the backseats. "The air conditioner doesn't work," she said as we buckled our seatbelts.

"We aren't going that far." I tried not to make a face at the awful pop music blaring from the speakers, but she must have seen my grimace. She laughed, the sound so light and airy, and reached out to change the channel. I touched her hand and shook my head. "Leave it. This is your car."

Before I even got us out of the parking lot, her phone was ringing. She dug it out of her purse and answered the call. When she started speaking perfect Spanish, I glanced at her with surprise. I had picked up quite a bit just being around Dom's family as a kid, but Jem spoke as if she had been bilingual since birth.

From the bits and pieces I could understand, I gathered it was her supervisor. The woman seemed to be encouraging Jem to file a complaint about the way she had been fired. Texas was an at-will state so I didn't know how that was going to work out for Jem, but if she had a paper trail, it would be easier for her to get the unemployment benefits she had earned and deserved.

Of course, one whiff of this to the gossip rag vultures

and Jem would be dragged through the mud. We both knew what had happened back in that hotel room was mostly innocent, but no one would ever believe us. I had fucked that up by giving her that tip out in the hallway. *What the hell were you thinking?*

I wasn't thinking. That was the problem. Jem had blitzed my brain so badly that I hadn't employed the usual caution that kept me out of trouble. Instead of hurting myself, I had hurt her. That was something I couldn't forgive or forget. I had to be more careful with her.

Everything Diego had said about me was true. I was a prick, and a nice girl like Jem had no business being anywhere near me.

But I couldn't stop what I felt for her. This connection between us? It was instant and *real.* This wasn't just lust. It was something else entirely.

And I wasn't giving up on the chance to keep Jem in my life without a fight.

CHAPTER SIX

JEM

When we reached his building near Discovery Green Park, I felt embarrassed by the state of my sad minivan with its peeling paint and broken air conditioner. Step didn't seem to care one bit. He drove up to the valet station as if he were behind the wheel of a Hummer, handed over the keys to the valet there and gave instructions for parking it.

With his hand between my shoulder blades, Step guided me into his luxury high-rise and headed for the elevators at the rear of the lobby. He retrieved a keycard from his wallet and his cell phone from the super tight pocket of his leather pants. After using the keycard to activate the private elevator, he dialed a number and made a quick phone call. As he spoke a language I couldn't understand, he rubbed slow circles on my upper back.

"A friend of mine is going to pick up your van," he said after tucking his phone back into his pocket.

I panicked. "I can't afford to—"

"It's my treat. It's the least I can do after getting you fired."

"Step—"

"Let me do this." He swooped down and kissed the protest right out of me. I didn't know how to react to this whirlwind—well—whatever this was between us. Relationship? Tryst? I didn't even know what to call this thing.

While I was still trying to figure out what we were doing, Step took my hand and led me out of the elevator and into his incredible apartment. The far wall was floor to ceiling windows with an incredible view of downtown Houston. I wanted to press my nose up against the glass and try to pick out all the interesting spots. I quelled that urge and followed Step into the kitchen. Everything was upscale and luxurious, from the professional grade appliances to the gleaming quartz countertops and hand-scraped hardwood floors.

"Have you had lunch?" He asked as he opened the refrigerator and peered inside.

"No." I placed my phone and purse on the counter. "I was running behind schedule so I skipped my usual lunch break and dove right into my second shift."

He shot me a look of consternation. "It's after three o'clock. You shouldn't go that far between meals."

I decided not to tell him there were days near the end of the month where I sometimes skipped lunch entirely, but he must have guessed.

With one hand on the door of the stainless steel fridge, he held me in place with his piercing gaze. "You were going to eat eventually, right?"

"Yes. I had a lunch packed."

"Everyday?"

I squirmed uncomfortably. "Usually."

"Usually?" He slashed his hand through the air. "That shit stops right here, Jem. If you won't take care of yourself, I'll start packing your lunches and making sure you're getting three square meals a day."

That protective streak of his flared hot and bright. I didn't know why it made my chest feel warm and tight, but it did. When was the last time anyone other than Benji had cared whether I was eating or getting enough sleep or feeling well?

Needing to push back, just so he understood I wasn't going to let him run roughshod over me, I asked, "How do you intend to do that when you're on tour?"

"Something tells me your little brother would love to earn a cool grand a month keeping tabs on you," he replied quickly. "A thousand dollars is a lot of money to a sixteen-year-old."

"A thousand dollars is a lot of money to a twenty-one-year-old," I grumbled.

He smiled and then ducked back into the refrigerator. "I don't have anything fancy in here. We've been traveling a lot and working in the studio so I've got the basics. How about pancakes?"

He could have offered me a frozen pizza, and I would have been just as touched. No one other than Benji had ever cooked for me. "Pancakes sound great. Do you want me to help?"

"No." He set out the ingredients he needed from the refrigerator onto the counter and then strode toward me. Using the toe of his black leather boot, he pushed a barstool away from the counter and then picked me up like a naughty child and deposited me right onto the low-backed seat. "I want you to sit here and rest. Would you like something to drink? Tea? Soda?"

"Soda, please."

He kissed the top of my head, grabbed a soda from a cabinet and a glass from a cabinet that he filled with ice. He brought them back to me and then got to work making us a late lunch. Feeling awkward just sitting there while he cooked, I sipped my soda and then asked, "Have you lived here long?"

"I bought this place about two years ago?" He whisked batter in a bowl. "I don't get to spend as much time here as I had expected I would. We were on tour all last year, and then I had that throat thing in the spring. We've been recording in Tor and Leif's studio in Sweden the last few months. The plan is to go on tour again right after the New Year."

"That's a hectic pace."

"Yes." He moved to the griddle he had been heating on the stovetop and began to drop dollops of batter on the hot surface. "We've been incredibly lucky that our fan base has continued to grow. Every time we think about slowing down, we hit a new surge of popularity. It's hard to say no to tours when your fans want to see you so badly."

"I bet." I ran my finger around the rim of the glass.

"It's a lonely life." He smacked the spatula against his bicep as he stood in front of the stove with arms folded. "I realize how crazy that sounds because we are constantly surrounded by people when we're on tour, but it's not the same as being surrounded by people who love and care about you."

"Like your brother and cousin?"

He nodded. "My brother is a SEAL so we don't get to see each other as much as we would like. When we do cross paths, it's for a day or two at most." He flipped the first three pancakes. "Our cousin was locked up on an aggravated robbery charge until earlier this summer. I came to visit him every six or seven weeks. One time, I flew from Tokyo to Houston and then right back to Sydney a day later to make sure that I got to visit him on his birthday. The jet lag nearly killed me."

"You must really care about him."

"Yes." His voice had grown softer so I didn't push. He plated the pancakes and brought butter and real maple syrup to the island. I hadn't ever tasted the real stuff, but I kept that fact to myself. In our house, the cheapest pancake syrup available sat on our kitchen table during a pancake breakfast.

Step sat next to me, his thigh touching mine, and dug into the tall stack of fluffy pancakes on his plate. I followed his lead. In between bites, he asked me about Benji. "Which high school does he go to?"

"He attends a magnet school with a STEM focus. He

wants to be an engineer or a video game designer."

"Yeah?" Step took a drink of his ice water. "A friend of mine designs video games. She owns a studio here in town. They started out on a shoestring budget, but she's gotten massively popular over the last few years. Maisie Fernandez. You might know her name."

"Wait. Is she the one who has that zombie video game? The one with soldiers and cyborgs and crazy red-eyes zombies?"

He nodded. "That's the one."

I made a face. "It's gross. Benji always tries to drag me into his games, but I can't handle them."

"Benji sounds like my kind of people."

"He definitely is your people. He was at your concert last night."

Step's brow furrowed. "I thought you said he's underage."

"He is."

His expression turned pensive and then he seemed curious. "Your brother doesn't have the same father as you, right?"

"Right." I took another bite of pancakes. "People always asked if we were adopted when we were younger because I'm, like, as white as they come, and he's half black. It used to upset him so much when he was little."

"People are assholes."

"Yes, they are."

Step sat back. "Does your brother have dreadlocks and a labret? Another piercing on his eyebrow?"

I lowered my fork. "Yes. Why?"

Step shook his head slowly and laughed. "I met him last night."

"You're joking."

"No. We had a run-in at Slaughterhouse. I was leaving with those—I was leaving, and he had gotten himself into some trouble with our security officer. I made sure he got his autograph and a free shirt and then told them to put him and his friend in a cab." Step drummed his fingers on the island. "Small world, huh?"

"Yes." I almost couldn't believe how our lives had started to intersect even before we met.

"Did he get home safely?"

"Yes."

"Good. I'm glad." Step drummed his fingers a little faster. "It's really not safe for him to be out that late."

I shot him a warning look, and Step held up both hands. "I'm not criticizing your parenting. I'm just saying."

"He knows that he did something stupid, and he knows that he's grounded now."

Step tilted his head and reached out to run his fingers down my cheek. "It must be hard to play the role of sister and parent."

I poked at the small bits of pancake left on my plate. "Some days are easier than others."

"Speaking as a little brother who made his older brother's life a living hell, I can tell you with certainty that Benji appreciates everything you've done for him, and he loves you for it. But he's young. And young guys? They do stupid shit. The best you can do is try to give him good guidance and be there to prop him up when he stumbles."

"I try." Not wanting to talk about the reality of raising

a younger sibling anymore, I changed the subject. "So, if you have this amazing place, why did you rent that hotel suite?"

"I don't bring women here."

His statement confused me. "Um…"

His hand settled over mine, and he drew my gaze. His bright green eyes searched mind. "Do you understand what that means, Jem?"

I gulped nervously. "I think I do."

"You think?" He flashed that devilishly mischievous smile of his and leaned forward. "I'm not doing a very good job if you only think you understand."

I whimpered and clutched at his shoulders when he captured my mouth in a decadently erotic kiss. He tasted sweet and hot, the sugar rush of maple syrup making my head spin. Our kiss grew frenzied and needful. No longer constrained by my fears of being discovered at work, I surrendered to the sensual wantonness he had awakened in me.

"Step!" I cried out in surprise when he slid his arms around me and hefted me right up out of the chair. He used his arm to shove his plate and glass out of the way. Silverware clattered when it hit the floor. The glass tipped over and began to spill water onto the floor. Neither of us gave a damn in that moment.

He deposited me right in front of him on the counter and forced my thighs open. After insinuating his body between my spread legs, he cupped the back of my head and ravenously claimed my mouth. I couldn't do anything but hold on tight for the ride as his tongue darted against mine and his fingers flicked through the buttons on the front of my uniform. He bared my cheap Walmart bra to his hungry gaze and then nuzzled his face between my breasts.

My head dropped back as he dotted feverish kisses on my cleavage and then along the sensitive curve of my throat. I had never experienced anything like this. My body trembled wildly, and I felt that slick, pulsing heat throbbing between my thighs. I clung to his shoulders and tried to slow it down, even if just for a few minutes.

"Wait," I panted in between frantic kisses. "Stop."

"What?" He teethed my earlobe, and I nearly slid off

the counter and right onto the floor. The sharp little bite of pain traveled right to my pulsing clitoris. I hadn't felt a jolt like that even when touching and exploring myself late at night.

"I've been working all day." I feebly searched for an excuse.

"And?" His lips were on the swell of my breast again. "God, you have gorgeous tits. I have to get you out of this bra..."

"Wait." I grasped his wrist. "I—"

He held still and waited for me to give him a reason why we had to stop.

I swallowed and licked my lips. "Um...I'm all sweaty?"

"Is *that* what you're worried about? Hell, that's easy enough to fix."

Without another second of warning, he stood up, collected me in his arms and tossed me over his shoulder like a freaking caveman. "Step!"

"You're the one who wanted a shower," he reminded me, amusement filling his voice.

Dangling upside down, I whacked his taut backside with both hands. "Put me down!"

He laughed and kept on walking. The floor in my bouncing vision soon changed from hardwood to marble. He carefully lowered me to my feet and stepped away just long enough to turn on the walk-in shower. I only had a few seconds to marvel at his gorgeous bathroom before he was standing in front of me and tugging at my clothing. His wicked kisses made my head pound—and before I knew it, I was stark naked in front of him.

Step breathed hard as he gazed at my body. He looked at me as if I was the most beautiful woman he had ever seen. "That's it. From now on, I shop for myself on my birthday because you are the prettiest fucking gift I have ever unwrapped."

I blushed hotly, but he tipped my head back with his fingers beneath my chin. "Don't be embarrassed, Jem. You are *gorgeous*."

"I…"

"You." He kissed my mouth. "Are." His lips danced

across my breasts. "Beautiful." He suckled my nipple and released it with a noisy pop. "You are beautiful."

He lifted his head and gazed into my eyes, and I felt all my inhibitions flee. I reached for his shirt and started to lift it up his chest. I was too short to pull it off of him so he took over and let me concentrate on his pants. Pushing aside my hands, he quickly peeled out of them and threw them across the bathroom. Naked and flushed, we stared at each other for a moment, both of us smiling nervously.

"Come here, *rybka*." He reached for my hand and dragged me into the shower. I closed my eyes and let him run his big hands all over my body. Pulling me back against his chest, he pointed at the tile in front of me. "Put your hands there."

I did as instructed, mainly because I didn't know if could stand up straight without the help. Behind me, he lathered up his palms and spread soap along my curves. I tried not to hyperventilate when he cupped my bare sex with his sudsy hand and bit down on the curve of my neck. His fingers traced the seam of my pussy. "I can't wait to get my tongue right here."

I nearly passed out when he said that. It was the dirtiest, most exciting thing a man had ever said to me—but he wasn't done yet.

"I'm going to bury my face in your cunt until you come and come and beg me to stop." His fingers swirled around my swollen clitoris, and I clawed at the wet tile, my fingers squealing against the marble. "Then I'll let you ride my cock. I want to watch you bouncing on my lap while I enjoy these." He cupped both of my breasts and then pinched my nipples.

I cried out and tried to catch my breath. My body was on fire now. I didn't know how much more of this I could take. Was this moving too fast? Did I need to put the brakes on? Maybe we needed a time-out. "We have to stop."

"You're right." Step dragged me under the water spray and rinsed away the soap clinging to my skin. "This floor is way too slippery."

"That's not quite what I meant."

Step silenced me with a kiss. Suddenly, I didn't care

anymore. The reasons we shouldn't do this fled. All I could think about were reasons why I *should.*

After hastily drying off, we practically ran to the spacious master suite. It was sparsely furnished with only a huge bed, a dresser and a chair. The place hardly looked lived in, and it made me sad.

"What's that look, baby girl?" He plucked the pins from my hair and set my long dark locks free.

"I was just thinking that you have this amazing life and all this success but—"

"But I have no one to share it with," he finished for me. Combing his fingers through my hair, he bent down and kissed me tenderly. "I'm working on changing that."

A tremble of something so powerful and hopeful rippled through my stomach. The idea that maybe I had finally found someone who wanted the same things I wanted was so incredibly seductive. But it was so early in our relationship, and I wasn't about to get swept away with what-ifs.

Centered in the here and now, I embraced the moment and let him guide me down to the bed. Step explored my body at a leisurely pace. I gripped the sheets beneath me as his mouth and hands discovered all the sensitive spots that made me gasp and shudder. His mouth trailed down my belly, and I swallowed hard. I thought of all the things he had described in the shower.

When he parted my thighs with his huge hands and gazed hungrily at my pussy, I turned bright red and tried to shut them. He applied enough pressure to stop me. "Let me look at you, Jem."

I closed my eyes and tried not to die of embarrassment as he used those big fingers of his to hold open the dewy petals of my sex to get a better look. I suddenly felt uncertain and shy. Considering I hadn't had a boyfriend since high school or even attempted sex since then, I hadn't exactly gone for a full Brazilian down south. I thought of the pretty, confident women he had been with last night. They probably knew all sorts of amazing bedroom tricks. Me? I hadn't picked up a copy of *Cosmo* in years.

"Don't be shy with me, Jem." He dotted ticklish kisses on my inner thighs. "You can tell me what you like and what to do. I want to know how to make you feel good."

Lifting my head, I opened my eyes and found him staring expectantly at me. Did he want me to tell him how I liked oral sex? "Step, I haven't ever…you know."

He seemed surprised. "Never?"

"I've had sex. Sort of," I amended and glanced away with embarrassment.

"Sort of?"

"I tried. Twice. It wasn't very good or very long."

"It wasn't very long? You mean his cock?"

My cheeks burned. "He was average, I guess. I meant the actual sex. The first time didn't last a minute. The second was a little longer." I shrugged. "I just sort of wanted it to be over so I didn't mind."

"Jemima." The gruff way he spoke my name surprised me. "Look at me."

I did. "What?"

"Do you want to be here with me?"

"Yes." I didn't hesitate because it was true. I wanted to be here with him.

"Do you want me to make love to you?"

"Yes."

Reassured that I wanted him and wanted this, he stroked his hands up and down my belly. "Relax, *milaya moya*. Relax and let me show you how good it can be."

Loving the way he called me sweet names in his mother tongue, I nodded and fell back to the bed. He growled something in Russian, his voice deep and low, and then he swiped the length of my slit with his tongue. My hips shot off the bed, and he grasped my waist to hold me down. His tongue probed my lips, gliding between them slowly and flicking gently at my clit. He suckled that little nub with a few long tugs and then returned to circling it.

I fisted the sheets and tried to catch my breath. Oh, God. Why didn't I know? Why hadn't anyone told me it could feel like this?

"Step!" I reached down and touched his hair as his tongue did so many wicked, naughty things to me. He probed my entrance, using it to penetrate me, and then swirled it around my clit until I was panting and aching and hovering right on the edge of something amazing.

One of his hands slid along my front and covered my breast. He found my nipple and pinched the stiff peak. The little twist of pain sent me into the stratosphere.

With a burst of pure bliss, I shouted his name and started to buck my hips. He was so much stronger than me that he easily held me down and kept right on flicking and fluttering his tongue. He slid a finger into me, curving it just a little, and stroked inside my slick channel until I was shaking with need. "Oh, God. Oh, God. *Please.*"

He growled against my pussy, and I came hard, even harder than the first time. Even with my eyes clenched shut, I saw brilliant starbursts as the powerful shockwaves rattled through me. Awash with ecstasy, I shuddered atop the bed and moaned as Step's tongue lapped at my clit. He pulled the tiny nub between his lips and sucked on it a few times. My legs started to wobble, and I thought I might be having a heart attack.

Showing some mercy on my poor, wrung out body, Step abandoned my pussy and kissed his way up my body. He spent some time fondling and nipping at my breasts before capturing my mouth. It was strangely heady to share something so intimate after he had been using that skilled mouth of his to make me scream.

Step trapped one of my thighs between his legs and pushed a second finger into me. I gasped at the sudden intrusion, and he eased off the force of his thrusting digits. Pulling back, he gazed down at me and searched for permission to continue. I nodded and reached down between our bodies to grasp his cock. The hard, hot shaft required both hands, but there was still more I couldn't cover.

He shuddered as I stroked him with both hands. The slippery drops of pre-cum dripping from the head of his cock eased the way. I watched his face for guidance and squeezed him tighter as I stroked up and down his shaft. Step's fingers kept working me, thrusting in and out at the same pace that my hands glided up and down his steely length.

When I slid a hand down to cup his balls, Step cursed loudly and crashed his mouth to mine. I took that as a good sign and kept right on stroking and fondling him. His fingers faltered, and I knew he was close. Thinking of the way he had used a little pain to heighten my pleasure, I bit his lower lip—and he jerked hard against me.

Hot bursts of ropy cum landed on my belly. I stroked him through his orgasm, rubbing my hand up and down his cock until every last drop had been milked onto my skin. He dropped down beside me like a fallen tree and buried his face in the curve of my neck. Wrapping his arms around me, he slung a heavy leg across mine and held me close.

We were cuddling contentedly when I heard my cell phone ring in another part of the apartment. Beside me, Step grunted. "Leave it."

"I can't." I pushed at the muscled arm embracing me. "It's my brother. He never calls unless it's important."

Step grumbled but loosened up his hold on me. "Come right back when you're finished."

"I will."

Even after everything we had done, I was too shy to run around his apartment naked. I yanked the top sheet off the bed and wrapped it around my body before fleeing the bedroom to find my phone. By the time I reached the kitchen and my purse, my cell phone alerted me to a voicemail. I swiped my finger across the screen and tapped in the unlock code.

When I got to the voicemail screen, I tapped the new message from Benji and waited for it to play. How was he going to react when he found out I was dating Step? Would he be excited for me? Would he approve?

"Jem!" Benji's voice came across panicked and frightened. "Jem, they're here! They're looking for Dad. Call me back. Now."

I did. I hit the button and gripped the counter. My quick run-in with Spider came to the forefront of my mind.

"Jem!"

"Benji! Are you okay?" In the background, I could hear someone beating on a door or a wall. "Benji! Hide! Go hide!"

"I can't. They're—"

A loud crash rattled my ear.

"Shit! Jem! They're in the house. Jem. JEM!"

Benji screamed—and the line went dead.

"Benji? BENJI!"

CHAPTER SEVEN

STEP

Wearing a dopey fucking grin, I stared up at the ceiling and enjoyed the post-sex haze of happiness. This was the first time since I had lost my voice that I felt complete and whole. Jem had given me my hope back. She made me feel as if I could slay a fucking dragon.

I was thinking of all the ways I could woo her old-school style and convince her that I wanted to pursue something real and lasting with her when I heard her panicked scream. I shot out of bed like a damned rocket and ran across the apartment. I found her in the kitchen frantically dialing her phone and starting to sob hysterically.

"*Rybka!*" I grasped her shoulders and gave her a little shake. "Look at me! What's wrong?"

"They took him!"

"What? Who?" I glanced at her phone. "They took your brother?"

"Yes."

I slid an arm around her shoulders and hugged her close. She was shaking like a leaf. "*Angel moy*. Calm down. Okay? Who took him?"

"The meth dealers Jackie crossed," she said with a loud sob. "The guy who owns our trailer park? His name is Spider, and he's the VP of the Calaveras MC."

"Yeah?" I didn't like where this was going. I hadn't been part of the Houston underworld since high school, but I still knew the major players. Spider and his men were allied very closely with Romero Valero, the man who had staged a coup against his old cartel boss only weeks earlier.

"Spider stopped me this morning when I was headed

to work and told me that he had heard that Jackie was back in town and that he had robbed some meth dealers. He warned me that they might come looking for Jackie at our house. I warned Benji to be careful—but I should have been there! I should have been there to protect him!"

The thought of Jem being grabbed by a bunch of loser meth heads and drug dealers chilled me right to the bone. Her brother would be safe so long as he cooperated, but her? Oh, God. She was just so damned sweet and tempting. Men like the monsters who had taken her brother couldn't be trusted around any woman, let alone one as innocent and gentle as her. They would have hurt her badly.

Realizing she needed me to be strong, I kissed her tenderly and then cupped her face. "I will get your brother back."

"How? Step, these people are dangerous."

"So are *my* people." I kissed her again. "We need to get dressed."

"Why? Where are we going?"

"To see my cousin."

Half an hour later, I glanced at Jem who sat stoically but teary-eyed in the passenger seat as I navigated the stately streets of Houston's oldest and wealthiest enclave in my matte black '60 Coupe de Ville. The estates here were owned by the most powerful people in the city, but I only cared about one of them—Nikolai Kalasnikov, the unacknowledged Russian mob boss and the most dangerous man in the city's underworld. If anyone could help us right now, it was Nikolai.

Luckily for me, Ten was working for the boss as a bodyguard for Vivian Kalasnikov, Nikolai's beloved wife. When we pulled up in front of the house and parked, Jem glanced at me with such anxiety. "Are you sure this is the right thing to do? What about the police?"

"The police are the last people you want to involve." I could see that she understood that, but she was so desperate to save her brother that she would try anything.

Gripping the door handle, she asked, "What is he going to want for payment?"

I leaned over and kissed her temple. "Let me worry

about that."

"Step," she said quickly. "You can't get yourself into debt for me."

"I can, and I will."

"Why?" She seemed bewildered by my decision to help her.

Now I was the one feeling anxious. "You know why."

The fear in her eyes faded, and she covered my hand with hers. "Yes, I do."

I interlaced our fingers. "Let me do the talking. This will be a tricky situation to navigate."

She nodded dutifully. "I understand."

Hand in hand, we made our way up the cobblestone sidewalk that led to a beautiful front porch and ornately carved wooden doors. The historic home had been carefully restored and was the jewel of the neighborhood. I had heard that Nikolai had even more beautiful gardens out back, but I wasn't close enough to his inner circle to have ever gotten an invitation. Right now, I was breaking a big rule coming to his house, but I didn't have any other choice.

Someone had decorated the porch for fall and Halloween with pumpkin displays and planters overflowing with burgundy and orange mums. A whimsical wreath featuring black ravens and what appeared to be pages from Poe's book adorned the grand door. I rang the doorbell and stepped back, making sure I was clearly visible through the glass. I doubted very many people were stupid or brave enough to walk up to this front door and knock.

The door opened a short time later, and I found myself staring down into the strikingly beautiful face of an obviously pregnant woman. With her dark hair in a high ponytail, Vivian Kalsnikov wore a simple dress in a color that reminded me of grapefruit. As expected of a perfect little mob wife, she looked primped and ready for a day of shopping or running errands. I couldn't imagine the weight of all the responsibilities and expectations resting on her slim shoulders.

I greeted her in Russian, and she returned it with a smile. I started to tell her my name, but she waved her hand and addressed me in English.

"You're Stepan, Ten's cousin. The big rock star," she added with a grin. "And who is this?" Her smile faded when she noticed Jem's red eyes and the obvious signs of crying. "Oh my goodness! What's wrong?"

"We need to speak with your husband."

"Of course," Vivian said and gestured for us to come inside. She shut the door and rubbed Jem's back. "I don't know what's happened, but if there is any way for my husband to help you, he will." She motioned for us to follow. "This way, please. Kolya and Ten are in the library."

So lost in her fear and worry for her brother, Jem seemed oblivious to the bodyguards eyeing us from the shadows of the house. I spotted a man younger than Jem and a man closer to my age lurking in doorways and following our every move. I tried not to let it bother me. The sort of danger that lurked outside the Kalasnikov's front door wasn't anything I could ever understand.

Vivian knocked on the door of the library and poked her head inside. She spoke softly to her husband in Russian, but it was Ten who yanked the door open and greeted us first. My cousin wrapped me up in his massive arms and lifted me off the ground in a bear hug that squeezed the air right out of my lungs.

"Why didn't you call me? You should have told me you were coming over. I would have been waiting for you." Ten gripped the back of my neck and grinned at me. His gaze slid to my left and settled on Jem's petite form. "And who is this?"

"This is my girlfriend, Jem." I stepped forward and lowered my voice. "We need your help."

Ten's pleased grin collapsed. He glanced from me to Jem and back to me. "I see."

"Jem?" Vivian stepped in and took charge. "Why don't you come with me? We'll have a cup of tea while they sort this out, okay?"

Jem shot me a questioning glance, and I nodded at her. She reluctantly let go of my hand and followed Vivian away from the library. Assured that she was safe here, I trailed Ten into the library. The door was shut behind me, and I found myself face-to-face with the man who held Benji's life in his hands.

Though not as tall or muscular as Ten, Nikolai presented an imposing picture. With his arms crossed, he leaned back against his desk and exuded an air of pure danger. This wasn't a man to be crossed. Whatever he asked of me, I had to be sure I could repay the debt—or else he would find a way to collect that I would not enjoy.

"Nikolai Nikolayevich," I greeted with respect. Though the man was known to be an orphan, it was assumed by everyone that his father had shared his same first name.

"Stepan," he said stiffly. "It's been a while."

"Yes."

The mob boss studied me intently. "You typically come pay your respects at Samovar. If you're coming to my front door…"

"I'm sorry. There was no time to do it properly."

Nikolai exhaled roughly. "What's happened?"

"My girlfriend's brother was just kidnapped by a bunch of meth heads. He's just a kid. I didn't know where else to go."

Nikolai stiffened. "Have you called the police?"

"No."

"Good."

"What's your girlfriend's connection to this mess?" Nikolai narrowed his eyes. "Is she a user?"

I shook my head. "It's her stepfather. He's not in the picture. She has custody of her little brother. The dad split town years ago, after the mom went to prison, but he's back now. She said that her landlord stopped her this morning to give her a heads-up that her stepfather was up to no good. Apparently, he robbed a bunch of meth heads."

"Who is her landlord?"

"Spider."

"I see." Nikolai's mouth settled into a tight line. "What is the stepfather's name?"

"Jackie."

Nikolai shrugged. "I don't know him." He glanced at Ten who shook his head. "Get Ilya. He knows everyone."

Ten left the room, and Nikolai stared at me for an uncomfortably long moment. "This girl of yours?"

"Yes?"

"You care about her?"

"I do."

"Does she know how to keep quiet? Because you know how I feel about loose ends," the boss warned.

Mouth dry, I nodded. "I do."

The door opened and Ten returned with Ilya. Once it was closed, Nikolai asked, "Jackie? A meth head? Dealer?"

Ilya nodded. "Yeah, he's from the Bloody Nick. He used to run product for Nickel Jackson, but he's been out of that crew for years. He has no protection. He has no backup. He's a freelancer and small time."

Nikolai nodded. "That's one less complication."

"Boss?" Ilya said hesitantly.

"Yes?"

"Stepan's girl? This Jemima?"

"What about her?" Nikolai asked, and my stomach clenched painfully as I waited to hear what would be said. Maybe coming here was a mistake. If she had some history with the family that I didn't know about…

"Her father was Crazy Kenny Coates."

Nikolai's face slackened. "Is Boychenko with Vivian?"

Ilya nodded. "I told him to stay close, just in case."

"Just in case *what*?" The fine hairs on my arms and the back of my neck rose on end. "Are you threatening Jem?"

"No." Nikolai spread his hands out in front of him. His calmness terrified me. This was a man who could shake your hand and smile—all while knowing a hit had been greenlit on your ass. "Your girl is safe in my home and in my city."

"But?" I knew there was more to this story, and I wanted the details now.

"Has she told you anything about her father?"

"She said he was killed by the cartel. She said that no one was ever arrested. There were no suspects."

Nikolai dragged a finger across his throat in the same way Jemima had done earlier in the day. "There's only one man who used that as his calling card when he was enforcing for the cartel."

The way Nikolai phrased his reply made my heart skip a beat. "Romero Valero? Vivian's father?"

He nodded. "So you understand why I'm concerned

about my pregnant wife sitting down for a cup of tea with the daughter of a man killed by her father, yes?"

"Yes."

Nikolai straightened up and walked behind his desk. "What I've just told you? It stays between us. Nothing good will come from telling our women that truth. It's old and dead and buried. Let's leave it where it belongs—six feet underground."

I didn't like it, but I knew what would happen if I ever revealed what I had learned here. Not even my connection to Ten could save me or Jem then.

Nikolai picked pulled a burner phone from a bottom drawer of his desk, powered it up and made a single phone call. I expected him to call Kostya, the notorious cleaner who handled the family's dirty business, but he didn't.

"Mueller," he said with the hint of a smile. "I think we need to meet. I have a proposition for you, and I think you'll find it's something you've wanted for a while now."

I had no idea who this Mueller person was, but I had a bad feeling I was about to find out. The promise I had sworn to my older brother Semyon about staying out of the underworld had just gone up in flames. For Jem, for her brother, I had no other choice but to suck it up and wade back into those murky, dangerous waters.

CHAPTER EIGHT

STEP

"This shit brings back memories, huh?" Ten asked as we sat in the front seats of a black SUV with darkly tinted windows.

"Not all good ones," I murmured, thinking of the stupid, risky things I had done when I was the same age as Benji. "Who is this Mueller guy?"

Ten pointed to the real estate sign in the front windows of the empty strip mall. "He's a hotshot real estate guy from Dallas, but he has a growing branch down here."

"What does a real estate guy have to do with your world?"

Ten reached for the water bottle in his cup holder and unscrewed the cap. "He likes to keep his white sheets on his bed, but he's the most racist motherfucker you'll ever meet. He runs the skinhead action in Houston now. He's quiet and all about business—and that makes him incredibly dangerous."

Fully aware that Ten's ideal woman was a big, bold black girl, I had an idea of how much he hated working with Mueller. Thinking of Benji, I said, "Jem's brother is half-black."

"And?" Ten shrugged and took a long drink.

"And your boss is asking Mr. White Supremacist to save him?"

"Like I said," Ten replied, "Mueller will do this because Nikolai will offer him exactly what he wants as payment."

"And what is that?"

"The green light to go after the meth trade," Ten explained. "It's the Wild West, but Mueller and his guys want to control it. The boss doesn't want blood in the streets, but this is a controlled way for Mueller and his boys to make a statement. They can get this kid and clean out the rat's nest of dealers and cookers who kidnapped him." He dropped his water bottle into the cup holder. "Everybody wins."

"And a lot of people die!"

Ten shot me a strange look. "*Bratan*, what the fuck did you think was going to happen when you asked a *pakhan* for help?"

He had a point, but it still bothered me. "This isn't what I wanted."

"You wanted to save your girlfriend's brother. That's what you're doing. Focus on that. Everything else? Push it out of your head."

Knowing what Ten had done in service to the family, I wondered how many times he had given himself a version of that advice. There wasn't any other way he could stomach the things he had done without some sort of mental footlocker where he stowed all those troubling images and memories.

Ten perked up and gestured toward the building with his chin. "Here we go."

I watched Nikolai and Mueller come out of the empty building with two of their heavies standing escort. Kostya paid little attention to the conversation between his boss and Mueller. He scanned the area around us, probably searching for cartel snipers or worse.

It was twilight out, and I could barely make out the shapes and shadows in the parking lot, but I had no doubt that Kostya could see everything. The rumors that swirled around the man suspected of being a former Russian spy claimed that he had all sorts of crazy cyborg-style implants in his brains and eyes. He was no James Bond, but the man was dangerous and ruthless.

"Looks like it's on," Ten said as he put his SUV in drive but kept his foot on the brake. He glanced at me while he waited for the small convoy to move out of the lot. "Whatever happens, you stay close to me. Semyon will gut me if anything happens to you."

He wasn't kidding about my big brother's overprotective streak. It was a trait that had always made me scoff, but now I considered what I was doing for Jem and her brother. Semyon didn't seem so crazy to me anymore.

Mueller and his men pulled out of the lot first. One of Nikolai's other captains followed close behind. Ten and I brought up the rear behind the boss and the cleaner. I didn't ask where we were going. I stayed silent and let Ten get his head straight. This was his world, and I was just the interloper. I didn't want anyone to get hurt, especially not my own family, so I decided not to get in the way, even if that meant keeping silent when I really wanted answers.

A long time later, we turned down a winding country road in the eastern part of Montgomery County. It was a rural area not far from Houston where ramshackle houses and rundown trailers with foil-covered windows were the norm. The abject and cyclical poverty in this area crushed the hopes and dreams of too many. It saddened me. I thought of the abusive, drunken father and the life I had escaped and the life I had created for myself. I thought of how damned hard Jem had probably worked to save her brother and give him a chance at making something successful out of his life. I hoped he understood the sacrifices she had made to give him a chance.

Headlights were cut, and we were plunged into darkness. The caravan of SUVs crept down the bumpy, unpaved road. Thick piney forests surrounded us. Apprehension gripped my gut. I wasn't used to this sort of life anymore. I had gotten soft and couldn't hang with these hard men.

The SUVs slowed to a stop. One by one, men climbed out of them and started arming themselves for what looked like a fucking war. Ten slapped my arm and indicated that it was time for me to join them. I hadn't fired a gun in years and hoped they didn't expect me to try to use one tonight. I would be a liability they didn't need.

The man named Mueller had shed his expensive bespoke suit jacket and silk tie. His sleeves were rolled up to his elbows. In the bright moonlight, I spotted the dark and ugly swastikas marking his forearms. He had more tattoos on his elbows and swirling up under his shirt. One of his men handed him a pump action shotgun. He rested the barrel against his shoulder and glanced around the group of men waiting to join him. "Are we ready?"

After a round of nods, Mueller led the men into the woods. Nikolai clasped my shoulder to keep me from following. "We stay here with Ten."

My stomach churned violently. I breathed as quietly and slowly as possible and strained to hear every noise. The woods were alive with insects and animals. My heartbeat ticked up a notch with every passing minute. What was happening? Was Benji all right? I thought of how scared he must be right now and how terrified Jem was back at the Kalasnikov estate. I swore then and there that those two would never know fear like this again. Not on my fucking watch.

The blast of a shotgun tore through the stillness of the night and startled me. I noticed that neither of my companions showed even the tiniest hint of being surprised. I could hear Ten working a piece of gum between his teeth as he stood beside me with his arms crossed. Nikolai had positioned himself a few steps in front of us. He seemed to be watching and waiting for something.

Two more shotgun blasts ripped through the night air. I swallowed and waited, straining to hear anything that might let me know if Benji had been recovered and if he was unhurt. I flexed my fingers at my side and tried not to fidget too much. How long had it been since the last gunshots? Five minutes? Ten?

And then, faintly but growing louder, I heard the unmistakable crunch of approaching footsteps. Kostya and Three-Fingered Arty emerged from the woods with a hooded and cuffed figure between them. He was thrust at me, and I realized it was Benji. The moonlight overhead illuminated Kostya's shirt just long enough for me to catch the glimpse of blood spatter on his clothing.

I started to reach for the hood covering Benji's head but Kostya stopped me. He wagged a finger and pointed at the SUV. I understood his instruction. Benji had to stay covered and bound until we were away from here. No eyewitness accounts. No loose ends.

I silently helped Benji into the backseat of the SUV and got into the front passenger seat. I waited for Ten to join us. I wanted to ask him what had happened back at the house, but I didn't. Sometimes it was safer to know nothing. Sometimes it was safer to stay silent.

Not a word was spoken until we had almost reached Houston. Ten pulled over on an isolated strip of road, and I climbed into the backseat with Benji. I carefully untied his hood and pulled the fabric gag out of his mouth. He had a bloodied, bruised lip and busted nose. "Are you hurt anywhere else?"

Benji shook his head. His eyes narrowed and then widened. "Holy shit! Stepan Vasiliev? What the hell? I mean—*dude*. Why are *you* rescuing me?"

I accepted the frighteningly sharp knife Ten had offered me and slit the duct tape binding Benji's wrists together. "It's a long story, kid."

"Well, I think I want to hear it."

"Probably not all of it," Ten replied with a smirk as he took back the knife and folded it closed. "I doubt you want to hear the parts about your idol climbing into bed with your sister."

"Ten! Jesus!" I punched my cousin's arm, but he just laughed.

"Wait. *Wait.* You and my sister? You and Jem?" Benji reached up and touched his head.

"Are you hurt?" Concerned, I leaned closer to examine him.

"No, man, but I'm wondering if maybe I have a concussion and am hallucinating this. Because you and my sister? That isn't possible. She *hates* your music."

Ten snorted in the front seat, and I whacked him again. Turning back to Benji, I explained, "I don't need another fan of my music. I just need her."

"But *how*? How in the hell did *you* meet *my* sister?"

"It's a long story, kid."

"Yeah, well, leave out the gross parts, okay? I don't need to know all my sister's business."

"Fair enough."

"We need to get moving," Ten said, his gaze drifting to the rearview mirror. "What's your address, kid?"

Benji rattled off the number, and Ten eased back onto

the highway. I stayed in the rear seats with Benji and gave him the PG version of my day with Jem. He wasn't happy about her losing her job, and he made damned sure I knew it. When I explained that she would be working for me, he seemed lukewarm about the idea. It didn't take me long to figure out that he was intensely protective of his big sister. I had gone from the rocker he had sneaked into a club to meet to the man who wasn't good enough for his sister in the blink of an eye.

When we reached the home he shared with Jem, Benji led me inside to pack some bags for them while Ten stood guard. We didn't have much time so I had to let Benji help me pack up the necessities for Jem. Though their house was tiny and old, the two of them kept it immaculately clean and had made it into a real home. I envied the coziness and their happiness together.

As I stared at some photos of the brother and sister on a camping trip, Benji came to stand beside me. "You two look happy in these."

"We've had some rough patches the last three years, but it's been mostly good." Benji adjusted one of the frames. "Jem is an amazing person."

"I know."

"Do you?" Benji scrutinized me. "My sister is the sweetest, kindest person you will ever meet. She gave up a lot for me. She gave up college and her dreams of having a real career. She works two and three jobs at a time to make sure that I can go to my magnet school and pay for my trips and clubs and project fees. And she, like, *never* complains about it. Never. She goes to bed at midnight and gets up at four to start the cycle all over again."

"I want to take care of her, Benji." I touched his shoulder. "I'll take care of both of you, if you'll let me."

"I don't think Jem wants someone to play sugar daddy. I think she wants someone who will be her partner and help her achieve her goals."

"I can be that person."

"Can you?"

"Yes."

"If you hurt her—"

"I'm sure I'll make mistakes, Benji. I'm sure that we'll

fight and argue about all sorts of things, but I will never hurt her. I won't hurt her physically or emotionally."

"If you do, I'll fucking end you, brah."

"I know you will." This kid would be a full-grown man soon, and I had no doubt that he would carry through with that threat.

"You two done with the heartfelt chat?" Ten poked his head through the front door. "Your nosy neighbor is making me nervous. If she calls the cops, I'm fucking out of here, and you two are on your own. My P.O. will bust my ass for breaking curfew."

"We're good." Benji grabbed his backpack and Jem's small suitcase and followed Ten out of the house. I turned off the lights and joined them at the SUV.

When we walked into the Kalasnikov house a short time later, Jem raced across the kitchen and flung herself at Benji. He caught his sister and hugged her tight. As she embraced her brother, she held out her hand and smiled at me. Feeling like a hero, I gripped her small hand in mine.

I didn't know what our future held in store for us, but

I believed it would filled with happy moments like these.

CHAPTER NINE

JEM

Needing to reassure myself that Benji was okay, I peeked into the guest room he had claimed and made sure that he was sleeping peacefully. I tiptoed quietly into the room and placed his inhaler on the bedside table before carefully retreating and shutting the door. After the stress of his ordeal, I feared his asthma would bother him tonight.

I tracked Step down in his bedroom. Barefoot and bare-chested, he wore only a low-slung pair of pajama bottoms as he sat on the edge of his bed and strummed an acoustic guitar. There were sheets of staff paper and a notepad covered in scribbled lyrics on the bright white comforter. He glanced up as I entered the room, and I froze. "I didn't mean to interrupt you while you're working. I can come back later."

He set aside his guitar and held out his hand. "Come here, *rybka*."

"Vivian told me what that means." I crossed the room and let him pull me between his open legs. "Little fishy? Really?"

He laughed and placed a noisy kiss on my neck. "It loses a little something in the translation." He kissed my cheek and then my mouth. "I could call you *zaichik moy*."

I narrowed my eyes at him. "Do I even want to know what one means?"

"You'll have to Google it."

I pinched him. "You aren't playing fair."

"I know, and I love it." His hands slipped under the hem of my nightgown. They glided along the backs of my thighs and didn't stop until he was cupping my backside. "Are we still driving out to Dayton in the morning?"

"We?" His question surprised me.

"Your van is in the shop. You need a driver."

"Oh. Right." In the chaos of the evening, I had completely forgotten. "If you don't mind…"

"I don't mind." He dotted soft kisses on my collarbone. "I'll probably just sit out in the car and work on some new lyrics." His mouth skimmed my neck again. "We may have to postpone our big date tomorrow night. I caught the tail end of the news. They said that tropical storm is probably going to hit earlier than expected. Apparently it's picking up steam."

"That's okay."

"I'll make it up to you," he promised.

Holding his handsome face in my hands, I gazed into his eyes. "After what you did for us today? You don't have anything to make up for, Step." I kissed him lovingly and ran my thumbs along his cheeks. "I'm the one who owes you."

His mouth slanted with a sexy grin. "I can think of one or two ways you can pay me back."

"Oh?"

"Yes, but first…" He shifted me aside and gathered

up his music and guitar. When the bed was clear, he dragged me close again and whisked the nightgown off my body. He tugged my panties down my hips and thighs and then shucked his pajama bottoms.

We moved onto the bed and began to kiss leisurely. Step's hands roamed my curves, cupping by bottom and squeezing my breasts. He wrapped his arms around my waist and hauled me tight against his chest, dragging me right on top of him. Our bodies aligned in the most deliciously tempting way. His cock stabbed between my thighs, and for the briefest moment, I seriously considered just sliding down a few inches and sheathing his shaft in my slick heat.

"We can't," Step whispered against my mouth. "I want to," he said with a groan. "I want to feel your wet pussy squeezing my bare cock—but I won't put you at risk."

"Have you ever…?"

He shook his head. "Never. I've always gloved up, but I still want to be careful with you. Besides," he swept aside my hair and bared my neck to his seeking lips, "you aren't on the pill are you?"

"No."

"Then we have to be careful," he repeated. Step ravished my throat, scraping his teeth over my skin and biting down gently on my jugular. It wasn't enough to draw blood, but it would leave a mark.

"Step!" I gripped his shoulders and bucked against him. We kissed again, and Step smoothed his hands over my body. Gripping my bottom, he flipped me onto my back and shoved my thighs open. I was still dazed by the sudden move when he started lapping at my core. His tongue zeroed in on the rhythm and pace that had driven me crazy earlier. He flicked at my clit until I was scratching at his arms and swiveling my hips. I came with a soft cry and pushed my pussy against his mouth, desperate to wring out every last drop of pleasure possible.

Even after I had climaxed, he kept his mouth on me. His tongue probed my entrance and swirled around my clitoris. He suckled my pink pearl and fluttered his tongue over it until my toes were digging into the mattress and I felt close to another climax. Strung tight and panting, I clutched at Step and eagerly anticipated another powerful orgasm.

But I whimpered in protest when he abandoned my sopping wet sex and crawled over me. He lingered on my belly and breasts, caressing and kissing and teasing my nipples until they were bright pink and puckered. I didn't have a lot of sensitivity there, but he seemed to have found a way to enhance the pleasure I did feel by tweaking and suckling me.

Wanting to make him feel good, I pushed on his shoulders and silently urged him onto his back. Emboldened by the way he looked at me and that hungry glint in his eye, I clasped his hands and claimed his mouth in an insistent kiss. He rolled his hips beneath me, and his thick, heavy cock smacked against my bottom. I could tell he was seeking stimulation. I decided to give him exactly what he wanted.

I slowly kissed my way down his body and settled between his spread legs. I didn't have much experience giving head, but I didn't think he would hold it against me. With one enthusiastic swipe of my tongue, I drew a low, rumbling groan from his throat. When I wrapped my lips around his crown and rolled my tongue around it, he pawed at the bedding and unleashed a string of Russian that sounded suspiciously like curse words.

He was so big that I couldn't take all of him. I bobbed up and down on the top half of his thick shaft and stroked the bottom half with my hand. Step moaned as I sucked the blunt head into my mouth and lavished attention on it. I cupped his balls and rolled them between my fingers. My tongue glided along the underside of his prick.

Step started to pump his hips and reached down to tangle his fingers in my hair. I let him take control as he sought more stimulation and depth. I relaxed my jaw and let him fuck my mouth. He didn't take it too far. I could tell he wanted to go deeper and harder, but he held back. He wasn't going to push me or hurt me. His cock plunged in and out of my mouth until he finally jerked free and shuddered.

"*Milaya moya.*" He grasped my arms and flipped me onto my back. "I need you."

"I want you." I did. I wanted this so badly. "Please, Step."

He retrieved a condom he had hidden under the pillow and quickly sheathed himself. Holding the base of his cock, he ran the fat head of it between my slick nether lips and gently probed my opening. "I don't want to hurt you."

"You won't." I wrapped my legs around his waist and dug my heels into his bottom. My pussy pulsed almost painfully now. "I'm aching for you, Step. *Please.*"

He didn't thrust into me but carefully and slowly pushed inside. He gave me time to relax and grow accustomed to him. Stretched and filled by his cock, I gasped when he was finally buried to the hilt. I closed my eyes and surrendered to his erotic kisses. He flexed his hips and fucked into me with short, easy strokes. Our tongues moved together at the same pace, and I clutched at his shoulders.

Step shifted his weight to one hand and reached between our bodies. He framed my clitoris between two fingers and rubbed tight, fast circles while speeding up his thrusts. He drove into me deeper and harder now. My mouth fell open as I cried out with sheer bliss. Everything was amplified. Everything felt so damned good. Hot and shuddering, I clung to Step and tried to hold off on my climax. I didn't want it to happen yet. I didn’t want this wondrous sensation vibrating through me to end.

When I came, when I tossed my head back and undulated wildly beneath him, Step let loose. He fisted his fingers in my hair and captured my mouth in a punishing kiss while thrusting into me hard and fast. "Jem!" With a growl, he climaxed. "*Rybka*," he murmured. "Baby. *Baby*."

Our bodies slammed together in a wicked dance that left us both panting and shaking. He slumped next to me and took care of the condom before curling around my body and holding me close. I ran my fingers over the tattoos on his chest and smiled happily as he caressed my arm and kissed my forehead.

"What did Vivian say to you when she hugged you right before we left their house?"

The memory of Vivian's kindness filled me with

warmth. "She welcomed me to this big, crazy, overprotective family. She told me that we always take care of our own."

Step smiled. "That was nice of her."

"I thought so." I drew my initials on his chest. Not wanting to get into a deep conversation this late at night, but needing to know something, I asked, "Step?"

"Yes?"

"What happens now? I mean, Jackie is still out there somewhere. You're going on tour in a few weeks."

"Honestly?" He trailed his fingers down my back. "I have no fucking idea how it will work, Jem, but I believe it will. I think we have something special."

Calmed and reassured by his response, I lifted up and kissed him tenderly. "Maybe we just take it one day at a time."

Step traced my lower lip and smiled down at me. "One day at a time, *rybka*..."

AUTHOR'S NOTE

Step and Jem's tale was first offered exclusively in the ROCKERS AFTER DARK boxed set in 2014.

A sequel for Step and Jem will be released in 2016.

ALSO BY ROXIE RIVERA

Her Russian Protector

Ivan
Dimitri
Yuri
Nikolai
Sergei
Sergei 2
Nikolai 2
Kostya – Coming July 2015
Alexei – Coming August 2015
Ivan 2 – 2016
Danila – 2016

Fighting Connollys

In Kelly's Corner
In Jack's Arms
In Finn's Heart

Debt Collection

Collateral
Collateral 2 – Coming Fall 2015
Past Due – Coming Winter 2015
Paid in Full – 2016
Down Payment – 2016
Final Installment – 2016

ABOUT THE AUTHOR

A *New York Times* and *USA Today* bestselling author, I like to write super sexy romances and scorching hot erotica. I live in Texas on five acres with my red-bearded Viking husband, our sweet, mischievous little girl and two crazy Great Danes.

You can find me online at www.roxierivera.com.